DISCARD

FINDING WONDERS

FINDING WONDERS
Three Girls Who Changed Science

JEANNINE ATKINS

ATHENEUM BOOKS FOR YOUNG READERS
New York London Toronto Sydney New Delhi

ATHENEUM BOOKS FOR YOUNG READERS

An imprint of Simon & Schuster Children's Publishing Division

1230 Avenue of the Americas, New York, New York 10020

This book is a work of fiction. Any references to historical events, real people, or real places are used fictitiously. Other names, characters, places, and events are products of the author's imagination, and any resemblance to actual events or places or persons, living or dead, is entirely coincidental.

For information about special discounts for bulk purchases, please contact Simon & Schuster Special Sales at 1-866-506-1949 or business@simonandschuster.com.

The Simon & Schuster Speakers Bureau can bring authors to your live event. For more information or to book an event, contact the Simon & Schuster Speakers Bureau at 1-866-248-3049 or visit our website at www.simonspeakers.com.

Book design by Debra Sfetsios-Conover and Irene Metaxatos

The text for this book was set in Goudy Oldstyle Std and Old Claude Std.

Manufactured in the United States of America

0816 FFG

First Edition

10 9 8 7 6 5 4 3 2 1

Library of Congress Cataloging-in-Publication Data

Names: Atkins, Jeannine, 1953- author.

Title: Finding wonders : a verse history of girls and science / Jeannine Atkins.

Description: First edition. | New York : Atheneum Books for Young Readers, [2016] | Summary: "A biographical novel in verse of three different girls in three different time periods who grew up to become groundbreaking scientists"— Provided by publisher. | Includes bibliographical references.

Identifiers: LCCN 2015036450

ISBN 978-1-4814-6565-6 | ISBN 978-1-4814-6567-0 (eBook)

Subjects: LCSH: Merian, Maria Sibylla, 1647–1717—Childhood and youth—Juvenile fiction. | Anning, Mary, 1799–1847—Childhood and youth—Juvenile fiction. | Mitchell, Maria, 1818–1889—Childhood and youth—Juvenile fiction. | CYAC: Merian, Maria Sibylla, 1647–1717—Childhood and youth—Fiction. | Naturalists—Fiction. | Anning, Mary, 1799–1847—Childhood and youth—Fiction. | Paleontologists—Fiction. | Mitchell, Maria, 1818–1889—Childhood and youth—Fiction. | Astronomers—Fiction. | Women scientists—Fiction. | Scientists—Fiction. | Sex role—Fiction.

Classification: LCC PZ7.5.A85 Fi 2016 | DDC [Fic]—dc23

LC record available at http://lccn.loc.gov/2015036450

For Sylvia Vardell and Janet Wong
with gratitude for all you do to
bring poetry, and sometimes
science, to readers

We especially need imagination in science.
It is not all mathematics, nor all logic, but
it is somewhat beauty and poetry.

—MARIA MITCHELL, astronomer

CONTENTS

Mud, Moths, and Mystery

Maria Sibylla Merian
(1647–1717)

The Artist's Daughter
❖ FRANKFURT, GERMANY, 1660 ❖

Maria Sibylla Merian lived at a time when few dared to use science, instead of superstition, to explain natural events. Maria saw past the stories she'd been told, becoming among the first to understand how caterpillars change form through the process of metamorphosis, and the ways these small animals depend upon particular plants.

The First Secret

Maria scrapes old paint off her stepfather's palette
so he can start again. A few petals fall
from tulips he's turning into a still life.
Maria leans close to watch
a caterpillar lurch across a leaf. She wonders
what it's like to navigate more than one pair of legs.

Andreas, the green-eyed apprentice, says,
Don't stare at shape-shifters. Those have horns!
He swipes the caterpillar onto the floor and lifts his boot.

Maria steps past an easel,
scoops the caterpillar to safety.

Andreas's eyes dim almost to brown.
He says, *Caterpillars come from mud
and can change form. That's suspicious.*

Maria has heard tales of boys who wake up
as wolves. And how even a good girl may turn
into a witch. That word sets hooks under her skin,

like the tiny barbs on the backs
of caterpillars' legs that help them climb.
No one in Frankfurt has been tied to the stake
since she was born, but Maria knows that in other
parts of Germany, girls her age are burned.
She slips the caterpillar back into the bouquet.

Evening

A trumpet blares from a church tower at curfew.
Maria hears the footsteps of the night watchman
beyond her bedroom window. His torch casts
a brief, striped glow through slats in the shutters.
Her sister, Sara, sets her clogs upside down by their bed,
a charm to shield them while they sleep.
Sara, who's seventeen and certain of much, lights
one candle. She reminds Maria, *Never burn three at once,*
which can summon wicked sprites or imps.
One flickering flame can warn of witchcraft.

Maria doesn't point out that any flame may sputter.
She used to admire all her sister's answers,
but now that she's thirteen, Maria appreciates
uncertainty. Questions aren't like maidens' ankles,
meant to be covered by long skirts. Questions aren't braids
to be pinned to the back of a head and forgotten.

Maria pushes away the bedding, smells linen
and feathers as a moth sky-sails
toward the candle flame. Its pale wings gleam

like miniature windows.

Maria slides from the bed to catch the moth.

She holds it in the nest of her twined fingers.

Moths may startle when she speaks,

unlike ants, who march between food and home,

or bees, who don't change course at the sound of a voice.

She flattens her palm, pulls open the shutters,

whispers, *Flee!* The wings stammer,

but the moth stays on her hand. Is the moth tired

or has she been trapped inside too long?

Rules

Papa holds his hand high in a blessing before breakfast.
Maria, her parents, sister, two brothers, and the apprentice
circle the table. Both her brothers and Andreas
are a little older than Sara, who boasts and frets
about her upcoming wedding. Their brothers talk
about work that will soon take them away from home.

Mama, her hair tucked under a creased white cap,
sets out sausage, porridge, and rye bread. She pours
fresh milk from a pitcher, cuts a clean line
through the crisscrossing crust of apple strudel.
She says, *Maria, please bring what's left to your uncle.*
Don't tarry. Keep your frock tidy.

Sara frowns at Maria's green stockings, already smudged
where they show between her frock and wooden shoes.
She says, *You're too old to crawl under gooseberry bushes.*
A fräulein should stay out of trees and keep away from mud.

Maria protests, *I find blooms for Papa to paint!*

If people catch you with creeping things or wild herbs,
they'll think they're for potions or poisons, Sara warns.

Maria tucks the pastry into a basket. She hates
how growing up means more rules instead of fewer.
She's supposed to walk slower instead of faster,
look around less instead of more.

She ducks under the sign of paints on a palette,
fills a bucket at the well near the shed where Andreas
sleeps in straw each night beside the chickens and pigs.
As Maria leaves the house, Mama kneels on the steps
and whisks a scrub brush through water.
Her arms move back and forth like a prayer's repeated words,
as if clean stone could keep danger from the door.

The Silk Mill

Horses clip-clop on stone streets. Wagons clatter.
Women wearing green aprons stand before stalls
selling cabbages, plums, cinnamon water, and cheese
wound with wax. As Maria gets closer to the river,
the blue shimmer of a dragonfly catches her gaze.
Elegantly armored ants, wasps, and long-horned beetles
creep or flit between gardens and walls.

Maria crouches to look in mud that may hide seeds
swept by wind or carried by paws, ripped roots,
or even cocoons that look like rolled, rotting leaves.
She's heard that witches can disguise themselves
as small flying creatures that curdle cream or spoil butter,
so are called butter birds or butter flies. She's never
seen signs of such. She often calls butterflies
summer birds, for they fly only during warm weather.

Maria straightens her back and hurries to the mill.
She scrapes her clogs at the door,
where good earth changes to unwelcome dirt,
and steps into the cocoonery. Boys push

wheelbarrows heaped with mulberry leaves.
Barefoot children sort them to make sure none wilt
or are spotted, then pile good leaves on slatted shelves.
There, caterpillars gnaw paths through green.

Older silkworms spin butter-colored cocoons,
which workers collect, then drop in basins
of bubbling water. Warmth softens the gum
and loosens silk strands, which girls snag
from the water with twigs.
They reel up strands to twist together. Down the hallway,
these threads are woven into cloth on loud looms.

Maria spots a moth fluttering near the floor.
She kneels and slides a finger under it,
curving her other hand into a brief home.
She carries the moth into the small room
where Uncle Hans works. He says, *Guten Tag*, and thanks
her for the strudel. His eyes land on her sheltering hand.

I like to draw moths, she says. *I know folks say*
they must know dark magic because most fly
only at night or are found near new graves.

Uncle Hans says, *Yet there would be no silk*
ribbons, stockings, or gowns without moths.

Where do the silkworms come from? Maria asks.
I don't see mud in the cocoonery.

We don't speak of those beginnings.
He glances at a silver bottle on his desk.

I want to know. She wishes her voice didn't wobble.

Then tell the workers I said you might take a few
silkworms and some mulberry leaves for them to eat.
You'll need to pick new leaves every day.
Watch what happens. Perhaps you'll see
how silkworms come to be.

Don't tell Papa. She lifts the basket
that held pastry, where she'll hide the gifts.

It's our secret. Uncle Hans looks again
at the shiny bottle, not much larger than a thimble.
Some beginnings can barely be seen.

Paper Houses

Hiding isn't hard in a house that bustles
as Maria's brothers prepare to leave on apprenticeships.
Her sister sews her wedding dress, layered
as a wasp's nest. Mama is busy with errands and advice.
No one notices
Maria creep up a ladder and push open the trapdoor
to the dim attic. Here she folds stiff paper or parchment
into small houses with roofs like turrets or tents.
She smuggles in fresh leaves and saucers of water
for silkworms who hunch and hobble
over their green suppers.
Their sharp-cornered mouths
shift back and forth like saws.

Between chores and lessons, Maria watches
silkworms devote days to eating.
She peers through a magnifying glass.
How do silkworms see, hear, and breathe?
Are they growing? Yes.
On the seventh day,
one slowly shrugs out of its skin. Is it dying?

No. The skin stretches and shreds
to make way for a bigger and brighter casing.
The silkworm goes on eating as it had before,
nibbling a leaf, avoiding the veins.

15

Trust

Sunlight slants across small clay pots of paint,
catches in poppy seed oil. This room at the front
of the house is both studio and shop,
where patrons sometimes stop in to buy pictures.
Here, Papa turns wildness into stillness,
showing flowers as if they'd never fade or wilt.
He patches leaves with green
rather than paint the holes left
where insects made their meals.
He hides signs of roots or dirt,
making it seem as if lilies,
roses, and *Butterblumen* begin and end as bouquets.

Andreas paints the backgrounds, as necessary
as the flowers in front. Andreas also draws maps,
which some gentlemen buy, or pictures
that show the city small and as if seen by a bird.

Maria coats a canvas with a paste she makes
from potatoes to stiffen and strengthen the cloth.
She wants to be in the attic, though she'd rather work
here than stitch, spin, sweep, or study proverbs.

The guild rules that girls can't be apprentices
or paint with oils, at least not pictures to sell.
But that law disappears under the command
that a daughter must honor and help her father.
When she was small, Maria dusted books here.
Some had pictures of tulips Papa painted for buyers of bulbs
who wanted to see what might come after patience.
Other books had been printed by her first father,
who'd died when she was too young to remember much.
She'd just learned to turn pages to pictures of plants
and animals, or maps, while her mother said, *Be careful*.

When the paste Maria painted on the canvas is dry,
she layers more over the linen's knobbly weave.
She smooths the surface with a stiff brush,
then the dried cast-off skin of a snake.

At last she hands the canvas to her stepfather,
the man she calls Papa, who's given her so much advice,
often: *Daughter, trust your own eyes*. She wonders
how he'd punish her if he knew what she hides now.

Caution

Where are you going?

Maria is stopped by her sister's voice in the dark.
She thought Sara was sleeping, and wanted
to go to the attic to see what the silkworms do at night.
Maria gets back into bed and lies: *I couldn't find
the chamber pot.* Sara turns over, swats at a moth.

Maria catches it. She brings it to the window
as Sara shuts her eyes. Maria loves
how most moths are covered
with soft brown, beige, or gray dust.
Unlike bright butterflies, who choose day,
many moths blend with the night. They hide
on the undersides of leaves or in holes in tree trunks.
Some fold and flatten their wings to stay safe
between windows and sills, doors and frames.
Or wings are disguise, with patterns
like the bark of trees or the eyes of owls.

Circles

In the attic, a silkworm silently spins
a silk cocoon around itself,
like a dancer twirling
or a baker frosting a tall cake.

Does the silkworm get dizzy,
making a spoon-sized bit of sunlight
where self and home are one?
Can watching what caterpillars become
show Maria where they came from?
How long must she wait
to see what will emerge?

Half a Conversation

Andreas looks up from his sketchbook,
and asks, *Where were you?*

Maria stays silent. She doesn't say she came from the attic,
where she used just two hairs of a paintbrush to show
the slivery stalks—not horns!—on a caterpillar's head.
Now she gets straight to work, shuffling stems, pinching
brown or bitten leaves off her father's bouquet.

Andreas's green eyes turn narrow, like a cat's.
He speaks of women accused of wreaking havoc
with owls or hawks, who turn people into goats,
gossip into spells, or sunshine into storms.

Such tales seem peskier than any small animals.
Maria swats them away, but still feels the sting.

Mixing Colors

Maria waves a paper fan over a damp painting
to keep off dust while it dries.
She'd rather see what's happening in the attic,
even if it's more stillness.
Good watching means waiting.

Andreas works on the cityscapes and cathedrals
in his sketchbook. He ties a string to a pin dusted
with chalk that leaves a line to mark the vanishing point.
He uses tricks of perspective to sweep away space
between eyes and what they behold,
marking walls and walkways with a light touch.
Any people are too small to see.

He props his sketchbook against his hip,
so it juts like the spar of a sail, and says,
If I sell another painting or two, I'll soon have enough
saved to go study masterpieces in Italy.

When an assistant leaves, Papa takes on another
fellow to cut canvas and paint backgrounds.

Papa gives the young men lessons in exchange
for this work and some payment, such as the barrels
of pickled herring that Andreas's father sends.
She wishes Papa would say, *Maria, you're help enough.*
Even more, she'd like to study ceilings and walls painted
by Michelangelo, and caterpillars found in other countries.
Are such warm waves of ambition signs she is wicked?

When Papa's painting is dry, Maria picks up a pestle
and chooses from pots of yellow pigments from Italy,
burnt orange from France, blue from silver mines in Saxony,
and carmine from beetles in the New World. Her arm aches
as she grinds bits of gemstones with wax and egg
to thicken into paint. She mixes purple from shellfish,
red from beetles' backs, and yellow from onion peels.
Dried safflowers and thistles glisten as she stirs
in tree sap, poppy seed oil, and a sprinkle of sugar.
Every twist of her wrist brings changes,
both mysterious and with rules she can learn.

Hands

Maria winds a small cloud of fleece
over the spinning wheel, which clatters as wool tightens
and twists into straight, strong strands. She works
between Mama and Sara, whose face is pale and calm,
almost as round as the embroidery hoop on her lap.
Sara lifts and lowers a needle threaded
with silk, stitching flowers, all bright blossoms,
no sign of stems, as if they never needed dirt.

Mama sews mustard seeds inside the hem
of Sara's wedding gown. She says, *Folks say*
these make certain a bride's voice will always be heard.

Thank you, Mama.
Sara turns over her embroidery hoop,
studies the knots and loose threads.
Maria, you might take more interest.
It won't be long before you're betrothed, though
it will be hard to find a suitor for a girl who can't tell
the difference between pretty and peculiar.

You're too young for courting, but you should care
for how you're seen. Mama touches Maria's hands,
still scratched from brambles and stained
with paint, the pale shades of bruises.

Papa needs my help. Maria stops spinning.

It's time he asks less from you, Mama says.
Her rising arm makes a crescent of space
as she hems a straight line, meant to be hidden.

Maria wants Papa to ask more.
Few girls can sweep or stitch
without their thoughts moving past brooms or needles.
Sara longs for a house where she chooses the linen and china.
Maria wants to know what's beyond all walls.

Flight

Under cobwebs strung between
the attic rafters, Maria is surprised
by a rustling like paper being ripped.

A cocoon darkens. A creature crushes
what once cuddled and bound her.
Shreds of split cocoon fall.

Hesitant, determined, a moth uncurls
four damp wings, spreads them to dry,
swaps stillness for soaring.

Another moth comes out of a cocoon,
beginning a brief life of mostly motion.
Close to the ceiling, the two moths meet,
then swiftly separate.

What coaxes them together,
then apart? Maria wonders.
She hears angry voices rise from downstairs.
Her heart quickens.

Are Mama and Papa arguing
about her? Do they guess what she's doing?

She shuts the paper houses.
As she hurries into the kitchen,
Papa shouts, *I'm leaving!* and dashes through the door.

Maria knows he doesn't mean forever.
He's made such threats before.
But Mama dabs her face with her apron.
As Maria hugs her, Mama whispers,
Are you going back to the attic?

Maria steps out of the hug, closer to the hearth.
She tastes smoke. *You've seen my paper houses?*

I heard a noise and thought there might be mice.
I brought up my broom, but something kept me from sweeping.
The world is filled not just with rules, but with mysteries
I'll never understand. My daughter might.

Please don't tell Papa.

Everyone deserves to have a secret.
Then Mama says, *Be careful,*
the way she did when Maria was small
and turned the pages of books
to maps of far-off lands.

Beginnings

In the attic, Maria uses her paintbrush
to sweep scat off the mulberry leaves. She finds
something smaller and paler than poppy seeds.
Are the silkworms sick?

As days pass, the dots darken
to gray, then black. Later, they split.

A caterpillar, thin as a scrap
of embroidery thread, crawls out,
sprawls into a new self.

Rules that once seemed solid
as the windowsill now wobble.
Maria looks past what she was told
and claims what moves before her eyes.
Seeing is more certain than words.

The Bottom Rung

Maria sits across from Uncle Hans in his office,
which is steamy from the vats in the mill
and loud with the clatter of looms. She promises
to bring pastry on her next visit, and describes
what she found. *The silkworms don't come from mud.*

He says, *Aye. Their precious eggs*
once were smuggled from China, hidden
in hollow walking sticks or parasol handles.

The young are no longer than an eyelash,
Maria says. *I saw them on a leaf.*
Could other caterpillars come from eggs?

I don't know. Perhaps you'll find out.
It takes a strong person to see past old stories.

Maria has been taught that everything
that creeps on Earth—ants parading
with blades of grass balanced in their mouths,
or wasps papering homes—

is at the low end of life's ladder.
Above them are dogs and cattle,
who come below ordinary people,
who are lesser than kings and queens,
who stand under only angels. Life has an order.

But could each and every ant, caterpillar,
or bee make possible the greening
of plants, the flowing of water, food
on the tables of everyone from the poor
to princesses and kings?

In the Open

Pails and tins clang as men call, *Sweet milk! Hot bread!*
Barley biscuits! Maria passes the marketplace,
pulls the hood of her cloak low, and peers into puddles
for creatures seeking water and the earth's salt.
She curls a finger so its pad touches her palm
and looks through this small circle at caterpillars,
to more clearly see the stripes, spots, legs, and mouths.
It seems likely that if one sort of caterpillar starts as an egg,
so would others. Maybe most don't crawl from mud,
which was never as terrible as she'd been told,
but just a name for the wet world.

She inspects cracks in walls, looks around woodpiles,
under leaves in a turnip patch
and the rotting bark of tree stumps.
Some cocoons are crumpled like bacon,
some smooth as a bird's belly.

Butterflies rustle up low winds,
twist and tumble into a glide.
Maria waves her net. She drops

caterpillars into a box she covers with gauze,
nestles another in a nutshell, their homes for now.

Do all kinds of caterpillars shed their skins
to make way for bigger selves?
Do all spit threads they spin into homes
the shape of date pits, then turn into creatures with wings?
If she can prove that these quiet creatures start as eggs
so small they could be covered by a needle's shadow,
would her father see the elegant spin, lurch, and flutter
of one sort of self becoming another?

A Girl's Education

Maria masters much at the easel, but in the kitchen
she repeats tasks and learns through blunders.
While rolling dough, Mama mentions that moist breezes
can foil the cook. *Taste depends on where the apples grew
or what the bees who made the honey ate.
The weight of a cook's hands makes a difference.*
When the dough slips under
Maria's rolling pin, Mama says, *Try again.*
Mistakes bring discoveries.

Did she forget salt? Leave the strudel on the rack
over the fire too long? Reasons for failures are found.
It's not witchcraft that sinks a cake,
but accidents or slipshod attention
to the width of a log or the height of a flame.

Teachers

Maria brings discarded scraps of paper upstairs.
Her eyes move as slowly as her hand
around a goose quill, and as certainly
as the changes she's come to expect
from cocoons propped against the paper houses.

Her gaze is first sturdy as a command,
then softens with questions. Beginnings
don't always suggest the ends.
Some dull-colored caterpillars change
into bright butterflies, while more-magnificent
creatures become drab when winged.

One time, black flies, instead of moths, exit a cocoon.
Other cocoons dry up. Some never open.
How much that is as still as a cocoon
is only waiting?

When quarrels downstairs grow loud enough
to cover noise here, she opens the shutters
to let in more light. She pushes them

to the walls so they won't rattle in the wind,
making noise Papa might hear. She's grateful
for everything he's taught her about painting,
but caterpillars and plants give lessons all their own.

The Open Window

The brass knocker raps on the door. Maria swaps her paintbrush
for a broom so the gentleman who steps into the studio
won't be befuddled by a girl who creates instead of cleans.
He admires Papa's work, then Andreas's drawings
of cathedrals and city squares.
He buys two of Papa's paintings
and a cityscape done by Andreas. After the patron leaves,
Andreas whoops, pockets a gold coin, and talks about traveling.

Papa opens his sketchbook, asks, *What else might you turn
into finished drawings to sell?* He considers pages
of drawings, stopping at one of their house.
The attic window is framed by open shutters.

Maria understands that Andreas could see from the shed
what no one could see from inside the house.
She presses her hands together,
the way moths fold their wings
to disguise themselves as twigs
or tuck themselves under peeling bark.

Once Hidden

Papa isn't fooled. He turns from Maria to the door.
Fast with fury, his footsteps pound on the stairs.
She follows him up the ladder, her chin near his boots
as he shoves open the trapdoor. She scrambles behind
the man who could have asked anyone to mix his paints
but chose her, and confided the secrets of colors.
Now his scowl sprawls as he surveys the clutter
of paper homes, which could be ruined with one stroke.

Excuses and lies touch her tongue,
but she says, *They're not fiendish or foul.*

They're small monsters who come from mud.

*If any come from wet earth, it's because the eggs
are buried to stay safe, like seeds.*

*Eggs! They're not chickens or birds,
and nothing like flowers. Destroy them.*
He starts to back down the ladder.

Anger tightens in Maria's throat.

Perhaps Papa won't listen, but would her dear teacher

see what she sees if she put it on paper?

She must show life circling from egg to caterpillar

to cocoon to moth-mother, who may lay more eggs.

She means to honor her father

but also all the mysteries of the world.

Metamorphosis

In a quiet revolution, Maria paints
on one piece of paper
first how a small egg breaks.
Then she shows how a silkworm wiggles out,
small enough so that she could fit within the half-moon
of Maria's smallest fingernail. The caterpillar eats
the eggshell, then the leaf where she lies.

After about seven days of scrunching and sprawling
over leaves, she struggles out of her old skin,
which splits and flakes
like the bark of a growing tree.
Four times she sheds skin that's become too small,
and starts again.
Every change is a new chance.

After casting off her last casing, the caterpillar
spits a pale-yellow gummed thread that
she loops as if tying and untying a bow.
Instead, she's made a home around herself,
snug and safe from rain and hungry birds or insects.

Her labor is hidden as she hangs
from a twig while the full moon slims
to a crescent and disappears from the sky.

At last the cocoon breaks.
Pushing past sticky strands,
a fragile self unfurls.
Soft, moist, a moth fumbles
then unfolds four wings that flutter,
making her own faint applause.

Maria cheers softly, too, as she paints
each stage of life on one page.
An invisible ribbon links
an egg smaller than the eye of a needle
to a caterpillar curling in on itself, like memory.

Portraits

Andreas rolls canvases to take on his travels,
when Maria brings her painting of the silkworm's
transformation into the studio. As Papa looks,
the lines by his eyes fade like a fan being unfolded.
He says, *You've seen a strange beauty I missed.*
Just don't let your mother know what you found.

Bless you, Papa. She presses her hands together,
vows that one day she won't hide. She turns to Andreas,
whose light hair brushes his shoulders as he bends
over her picture. He lifts a finger to touch the cocoon,
which twists around the end of one sort of life
and the beginning of another.
His eyes are wide, not at all like a cat's,
as he says, *I'm sad to leave, Maria.*

Her name in his mouth warms her.
She nods, though she thinks parting must be easier
for the one going somewhere. They exchange a glance,
swift and silent as two moths meeting in midair.

Wind and Water

Standing on the wharf, Maria and Papa call
Godspeed to Andreas. He's on a boat on a river
that will spill into wider water, then the salty sea.
Maria wonders what it would be like to stand under sails
or ride in a coach behind horses on mountain passes,
or find caterpillars she's never before seen among olive trees.

Papa's eyes settle on the water. He says,
I'm going away soon, too. I want to paint more
than what's in one city. Different flowers.
And meet new people to buy my paintings.

Maria's breath catches as if she were punched.
She nearly loses her balance, but she's not a little girl:
she won't reach for her father's hand. *Are you leaving*
because I keep caterpillars? She bites her lip
so she won't say that she'll stop. *Are you ashamed?*

I've taught you everything I know, he says.
If you can show character in the back
of a caterpillar, you can paint anything.

Hearing the clatter of wagons and wheelbarrows,
water lapping against the wharf,
Maria steps closer to the disappearing boat,
which now looks the size of her hand.
Sails fill with wind, rustling like the ripping
of cocoons when what was once content
becomes desperate for sky.

Becoming

Mama quietly helps Maria bring the caterpillars
and their homes down to the studio,
where she can watch them more closely.
But after dark, Mama refuses to light even a single candle,
frets about money, sobs, *How could he leave us?*

She sells some china, silverware, and books.
Uncle Hans makes sure they have firewood and food.
Still, Maria is hungry. Her clothes feel too tight,
but she can't help growing. As snow falls
on the green shutters of brick houses, she cries,
missing her father and sister, who is now married
and with child. The scraping of skates on the frozen river
is louder than clip-clopping horses in the marketplace.

Another winter passes, then spring, when buds uncurl
into leaves, and mud is most fragrant. Mulberries turn red.
By the second summer Papa is gone, Mama asks Maria
to take down the sign with a paintbrush and palette
that hangs over the door. Mama says, *We have nothing for sale.
I should have learned to paint. It's not against the law
for a painter's wife. Weren't we happy? What will we do?*

Papa is still gone when Maria turns fifteen, then sixteen,
but Sara visits from her elegant neighborhood,
bringing baskets of food she pretends are gifts,
not necessity. Fear creeps through night,
but during the day Maria works, becoming who she must be.
She crawls under bushes and wades by the river,
looking for small creatures to bundle in soft leaves
and carry home. She paints caterpillars
decked in halos of bristle and fluff
within circles smaller than copper coins,
along with their green suppers, beds, and roofs.
Beauty has no borders. It includes tangled roots,
thorns, and nibbled leaves among bright petals.

A Return

The door shut three years ago by her father
opens. Andreas enters, taller, with wide shoulders
and a pale-brown beard trimmed to a point.

Guten Tag! Or do you say buongiorno?
Maria stumbles over the words, conscious
of the years and land that have come between them.
She puts down her brush, its tip still bright
with enough paint for two silver-gray wings.
She says, *My father isn't here.*

I was looking for you. As his eyes shift from her
to the work on the easel, the green of them darkens
to the color of the underside of mulberry leaves.
He unrolls his maps with rivers thin as thread,
and the Atlantic shown half the size of her hand.
In one picture, a whole city looks as if it could fit on a leaf.
He shrinks what's huge, while she makes small lives
larger so people can see more.

On the back page of his sketchbook he's drawn
a girl with hair braided like hers,

holding a paintbrush. She's bent
over a caterpillar taking shape on the paper.
He says, *I didn't forget you.*
He gives her a fistful of wildflowers.

They're beautiful. She feels the warmth of his hands
still on the stems of daisies, bluebottles, and *Butterblumen.*

Like you, Maria.

She blinks, bewildered by the promise
her eyes give without her permission.

A Bouquet of Caterpillars

Andreas is courting me, Maria tells her mother and sister,
who's visiting with her baby from her house across the city.
Sara says, *He's tall with fine eyes, but an artist
won't have money for bracelets or a silver door knocker.*

I don't care what's on my wrists or door, Maria says.

I wish we could afford to ask if you love him, Maria,
Mama says. *We can't keep this house much longer.
Just as you need a husband to lawfully paint
now that your father is gone,
Andreas needs a wife.
Only married men are allowed to join the art guild.*

She goes to the kitchen and returns with a thimble
full of mustard seeds she sprinkles onto Maria's palm.
I'll hem them into your dress. I wish I had more to give.
Mama dips her nose toward the flowers from Andreas.

Maria admires two caterpillars who nod
as they nibble a leaf.

She says, Mama, you allowed me to stretch
the rules that you believe matter.
Papa taught me all about paints.
No daughter could want more.

After the Wedding

Maria pulls down the garlands in the parlor.
Andreas's hair smells like honey as he kisses
her and takes her hand. They weave fingers tightly,
but still loose enough to move.

In their new house, Maria and Andreas arrange two easels
and tables they cover with jars of crushed rocks,
broken roots, abandoned shells, and dried blossoms.
She mixes these with oils for Andreas,
though she must use watercolors.
Women's work can't be hung on walls,
so she paints flowers and insects on tablecloths
or for books sold as embroidery patterns.

Neighbor children bring her cups of caterpillars they find,
though some mothers warn them to stay away.
They find it peculiar that carpenters come to call
with worms once hidden in wood, and farmers carry
caterpillars from garlic fields outside the city.
They say that she's too fond of moths, which they try
to drive from chests of woolens and bins of flour.

Maria ignores the gossip. She fixes a room upstairs
for her mother, who helps Maria give birth to a daughter.
Mama watches the baby, Johanna, as Maria paints
blooms that become background, making way
for the scuttle, scurry, or soaring of small animals.

For nine years, Maria prays for a second child.
Neighbors whisper that she must be bewitched,
cursed for being too familiar with creatures
meant to stay in walls or woods.
Andreas sometimes says that, too. He wants a son.
At last Maria's belly curves, turns taut as a cocoon.
She bears a second child she names Dorothea.

The grandmother sings to the girls in the garden
and washes the stone steps each morning,
as if a scrub brush might hold back harm.
Maria teaches her daughters to read, write, and stand
patiently before cocoons the colors of the moon,
and paint the gleam of scales on wings.

Two Directions

Not many people buy cityscapes or maps.
Andreas's work doesn't sell well. More people want
Maria's paintings of blooms or butterflies caught
in midflight, though most overlook
that she shows the leaf and stalk that were home
before a caterpillar wound a way into darkness,
then broke through its cocoon and claimed the sky.

Andreas measures the slight distance
between their fame and believes
he is cheated. Stinging words are spoken.
As a moth batters against a window,
Maria considers the need for a safer place.
She brings Johanna, now seventeen, and Dorothea,
who is seven, with her to a community devoted
to prayer and good work. She abandons the name
she used as a wife for the name she had as a child,
signing her work *Maria Sibylla Merian*.
She continues her studies, noting how moths lay eggs
on leaves that provide the favored food of the newly hatched.
She paints flowers, ferns, and small animals with such detail

that some bring them as guides to meadows or woods.
Her art is science, which wants questions as much as answers.

Her hair is gray as a wasp's nest when Johanna
marries a merchant and moves to Amsterdam.
Johanna writes letters about her husband's work
trading goods to bring Suriname's sugar to Holland.
Soon, Maria and her younger daughter
also move closer to the sea.

Another Country

In Amsterdam, no laws forbid women
to paint and sell their work.
No one has been burned as a witch for almost a century.
Days in this city seem longer, with no curfews called at night,
but lanterns blazing over cobbled streets and curved bridges.
Canals connect to the sea, where ships bring
people of varied beliefs from many countries.

Maria is welcomed into the homes of wealthy traders,
city leaders, and scholars who talk about how telescopes
and microscopes reveal new truths. They spin new globes
painted with fewer guesses. Some gaze into *Wunderkammern*,
curiosity cabinets crammed with rare stones,
seashells, stuffed hummingbirds, preserved beetles,
or displays of butterflies and moths no longer breathing.
Maria wants to know what these creatures ate when alive.
Where did they sleep? How high did they fly?
What's pinned and preserved can't answer her questions
about where they came from and how they changed.
She wants to see them in flight.

What She Is Told

Women don't cross the ocean,
at least not unless married to merchants or missionaries.
No one has sailed to another continent
just to look at and draw small animals and plants.
Some travel to claim land for kings, find treasure like gold,
or collect bark, berries, and pods to spice cakes.
But no one has sailed from sheer curiosity about the world.

Voyagers are in danger of shipwrecks, hurricanes,
sea monsters, or fires from lanterns tipped by high waves.
Those who survive under sails may die of peculiar fevers
in the New World. They might be eaten by jaguars.
Maria is told, *You're too old. You can't go alone.*
But nothing will stop her now.

Sailing

Maria's hands are still scratched from briars,
and now that she's fifty, webbed with wrinkles.
She sells paintings and borrows money to pay the fare
for herself and Dorothea, who agrees to come along to seek
insects that don't live in Europe.
They pack pea jackets, kettles, pickaxes,
boxes of caterpillars and aspen leaves for them to eat.
Maria writes her will.

She won't sail to North America, where, she is told,
women were recently hanged as witches in a village
called Salem. She and her daughter board a ship
bound farther south, to Suriname. They'll take their chances
on storms, scurvy, mouthrot, pirates, thirst, and theft.

Blue, gray, green, and white waves rise,
spill, and spin like huge cocoons.
While Earth turns toward twilight,
she spreads her arms to feel the wind.

The New World
1699

Maria and Dorothea first stay at a plantation,
but workers there seem too busy tending
to sugarcane to care about the forests beyond.
The mother and daughter fill rucksacks with tins
of watercolors, stacks of papers that curl
in the moist heat, butterfly nets, magnifying glasses,
a ball of string, beeswax, axes, and a gun.
They follow guides who chop paths through
tangled vines that choke shrubs and saplings.
The rich earth smells both sweet and spoiling.
Prickly or sun-colored fruit appears within arm's reach,
but many trees are too tall to see the tops from beneath
the lush growth, where, judging from the size of fallen
petals, flowers as big as plates seek sunlight.

Sweat pastes Maria's dress to her ankles, though
its cloth still snags on thorns, thistles, or roots
too stubborn to stay underground. Snakes as thick
as men's arms dangle or drop from branches.
She stops to paint tree boas, enormous cockroaches,
electric eels, snakes that rattle, spiders with sprawling legs.

Fog lifts, smelling of wild grapes, jasmine, and vanilla.

Questions twist together visible and invisible worlds,

turn her hand as Maria Merian paints

what has never before been shown on paper:

the curves of antennae,

curling animal tails, coiling snakes,

and metamorphosis—circles of change.

Blue Butterflies

What looks like danger may be wonder in disguise.
Maria's paintbrush drifts, but her intent
is as fixed as moths seeking sunlight.
She hears the drum and crackle of insects
eating leaves, shrieks of bright birds, snickering monkeys.
She rolls her paintings to load into canoes
along with chrysalises she hangs from branches
by her side, like poles without flags.
As the guides push off with paddles through muck
thick as cake batter, she watches
for signs of cocoons breaking open.

The hot air dims under leaves larger than hats.
Paddles slog, skim, or snag weeds, rotting branches,
and rough vines. The current quickens.
The river widens. She sees sun again.
Butterflies and moths wing-beat among blossoms
and leaves that bend with green grace.
The Arawak guides shove away sprawling vines
with paddles. They swing hatchets
to chop fallen trees stretching across the river.

The canoe glides ahead, then teeters.
Dorothea grabs her mother's hand
as water splashes over one side.
A guide struggles to right it.
Another raises a paddle.
Another shouts and readies a spear.
Maria gasps as a crocodile lifts its snout,
opens its mouth, revealing sharp teeth,
then slips back under the murky water.

The guides keep paddling.

We shouldn't have come, Dorothea says.

Maria takes back her hand, wipes her forehead,
and shakes her head. Science is made of certainty,
but welcomes surprise.
She opens her paint box
to sketch a mint-colored chrysalis,
smooth as a teardrop, that swells and splits.
Papery shreds fall,
but enough remain
for the new butterfly

to clutch while her crumpled wings
bloom like a ball gown midtwirl.

The butterfly lifts and fans her wings,
sky-colored on top, earth-toned beneath.
She rises and disappears.
Maria knows she's not gone,
but only blends with the sky's shimmer and blue,
sweeping stories beyond what can be seen.

Secrets in Stones

Mary Anning
(1799–1847)

The Carpenter's Daughter

LYME REGIS, ENGLAND, 1809

Mary Anning was born more than a century after Maria Sibylla Merian, when science was gaining ground. Most people now understood that butterflies began as eggs, but there was still controversy about the origins of life on Earth. Mary Anning discovered patterns in stones, fossils that often showed that animals no one knew had existed had lived long ago in the sea or on land.

The Promise

Rain falls. Gray sky, sea, and stone
blur into one. Mary walks
just behind her father, watching
for slippery stones and waves that might sweep
the shore and leave no place to stand
between salt water and cliffs too steep to climb.
Pa wants her to be safe. She wants him to be proud
of her, finding what they call curiosities: stones
with pictures of creatures or plants that seem
scratched by impossibly sharp needles or nails.

Mary and Pa stop at a stone marked with a profile
of a fish. They take out their tools and crouch to cut
the curiosity from the plain rock around it.
Their backs curve over their work like umbrellas
they don't own. Pa's hands are as steady
as they are when he straightens the sides of planed wood,
fitting joints for the corners of his cabinets. At last
he unbends and puts the saved stone in his satchel.
He faces the darkening cliffs instead of the way
toward home and says, *I'll look just a little more.*
All this rain might wash away dirt covering a wonder.

I'll come, too. She wipes her wet face with her wet hand.

Go home. Mind your step, Mary, Pa says, as if
she weren't ten and always careful. *I'll be back soon.*

Bean Soup

The soup that's hung too long over the hearth
smells in danger of burning. The Annings have no beans
to spare, but Mum won't move the pot
from the fire any more than admit
she's worried that Pa is so late for supper.
To let the soup cool might seem like giving up on him.

Mary and her older brother, Joseph, stack driftwood.
Their little brothers play in the washtub, pretending
to paddle through a sky of strangers' damp shirts,
petticoats, and socks strung between chairs to dry.

At last Mum ladles the soup.
She says, *When your pa saw night coming,*
maybe he stopped somewhere for shelter.

Maybe sounds as soothing as a smooth
stone, but Mary knows Pa is more likely
to cast his eyes down than up, searching.

After Supper

Mum tells the little boys to kneel and pray.
Be kind. Tell the truth. She murmurs, *All will be well,*
and tucks the baby, who's coughing, in an open drawer.
Rain pounds the thatch roof, splatters on cobblestones.
The racket is as loud as the waves,
which are steps from their walls. Their crash
scrapes the air with no lull between rise and fall.

Mary chooses a curiosity with an impression of a seashell
from a pile by the hearth. She wields a needle
to scrape dirt from spiraling ridges that are narrow
as the wrinkles of an old woman's neck.
She polishes the curiosity with a cloth, though
it's too dark now to see any shine on stone.

Morning

It's nearly dawn when Pa opens the door,
dragging a bent foot. His shoulder is smashed.
He cries out as he slings an arm over
Mary's shoulder so she and Mum can guide
him past the laundry line to bed.
She takes off his boots, their patches torn,
the fasteners mangled. One foot is crumpled,
perhaps beyond use.

Mum wipes blood from his hands and says,
Fetch the doctor, Joseph.
When she doesn't add words about how the doctor
is a thief for what he charges, Mary grows more scared.
She thins yesterday's soup, which Mum tries to feed Pa,
holding the tin spoon as she does for the baby.

Pa's breath and words have sharp edges
as he tells about the cliff crumbling
under his feet, the long fall.

Seeking

As Pa tries to sleep, Mum says, *Yesterday a sparrow*
got in the house, which means bad news ahead. That's over
now. Your pa will be fine with the right teas and rest.

Mary is used to walking beside or behind Pa,
as familiar with his worn boots as his face. It hurts
to see him lying down during this gray daylight.
As she tosses a pick, chisel, and hammer into her rucksack,
Mum says, *You mustn't go out. Not on those slippery rocks.*

I'll mind my step and look for stones to sell. We'll need to pay
the doctor. Mary ducks under the doorframe where Mum hung
dried elder branches to protect them from wicked spirits.

Mary strides past boats turned over and tied down.
The rain is no longer so fierce, but fishermen
must be sticking by their home fires.
She won't waste a storm.
Downpours wash sand and seaweed off curiosities
that rich folks on holiday might buy as keepsakes.
A good sale can pay for several suppers. Maybe medicine.

Rain pelts Mary's eyelids, blurring the cliffs,
drenching her shawl, thin dress, and stockings.
Sea collapses and smacks land. She finds
broken bits that make her wonder
about what's missing, but they can't sell
what doesn't look whole. She crouches
to chip loose a stone stamped with spirals.
These snakestones look like serpents wrapped around
themselves, curled like cats or a nest.
Each fetches a shilling or two,
which is about what Mum earns in a week doing laundry.
Some are as big as a grown man's bottom, though
this one is slightly smaller than her hand. Some folks say
they bring good luck, while others claim they turn people
first to snakes, then stone. Pa calls this nonsense.
None have heads, and he's sawed some in half,
showing whorls never seen inside a snake.

Mary chisels.
Her hands are red and cold.

Stone Gardens

At the round table by the door of their cottage and the shop
where Pa is now too weak to build cabinets or chairs,
Mary sells cockles, stone sea lilies, cupid wings,
devil's toenails, ladies' fingers, thunderbolts, and
what some say are dragon bones or verteberries, rounded
knobs crimped in the middle like the edge of a pie crust.
She scrubs stones shaped like teeth or bullets, or
imprinted with lines like ripples left by waves in sand.

She and Pa found these along the shore,
which neighbors call stone gardens.
They say that just as the good Lord created flowers
to ornament Earth, He sculpted a glorious underworld, too,
revealed by waves or wind breaking rock.
Instead of bright blossoms, these are the colors of shadows.
Others believe swirl-marked stones fell from the sky
on moonless nights, appearing without warning,
like the ferny patterns that coat frosted windows in winter.
Such tracings appear as mysteriously
as ideas find shape in words.

Some people say it's best to stay away
from puzzling stones, but others want them
to decorate bookcases or mantelpieces.
At the round table, Mary meets doctors and professors
from London who call what she sells *fossils*
and claim they're more than tricks of nature.
They buy them for curiosity cabinets, where nests,
eggshells, and pinned butterflies are lined on shelves
like questions no one knows how to ask.

The Village

Mary keeps an eye on her little brother as he rolls stones
like marbles, or pretends to be a dragon, then waves a stick
as a sword to slay one. Her best friend stops at the round table
to play cat's cradle. Sarah Jane lives up the hill in a house
with a yard of juniper and sea holly. She likes
to sit here to listen to waves when there's wind
or taste salt in the air when it's foggy.

Sarah Jane makes up stories
about the mill and quarry workers,
the servants on errands at the boot-maker's or apothecary.
She admires ladies wearing elegant gowns and gentlemen
decked in freshly brushed jackets that aren't thin at the elbows.
Most are guests at the Three Cups Inn, here to breathe
sea breezes or ride the donkey-pulled bathing machine
into the cold water, play cards or dance in the assembly room.

The Annings can no longer afford to pay for the church school,
so while Sarah Jane studies, Mary learns to be alone,
with just the company of bees diving into patches of clover
or chamomile. She looks over the thatched roofs of cottages,

stone barns, and the butcher shop. She keeps her eyes off
the pillory and stocks across the way, by the jail,
where people who owe money are locked up.
Will her sick father be put behind bars,
the rest of the family sent to the poorhouse,
never again to see sky or stand on stone?

Struck

Mum gathers bee balm, foxgloves, and thistles
to make tinctures and teas she says will help
Pa breathe easier or tame his aches. She is careful
not to disturb spirits by spilling salt, dropping a knife,
or setting a loaf upside down on the table.
She holds up an apple cut in half,
showing how her knife didn't slit a single seed.
That means blessings are coming. She scoops
out bits of the soft apple for the baby, feeds
him wedges curved like half-moons.

Some say lightning strikes witches, but Mum believes
Mary was lucky back when she was a baby
at a fair where, though clouds gathered, no one wanted
to leave before finding out who won a raffle
for a copper teakettle and roasted leg of lamb.
Then thunder rumbled. Lightning split stone-colored sky.
An old elm blazed. Bark seared and scattered.

Does Mary remember her small body burning
like an oven until her mother dunked her

in a laundry tub of water?
She can't always tell memories from stories
or even good fortune from bad,
not at first.

What Matters

Come summer, Mary and Joseph walk past the quarry.

He waves to friends smashing stones,

which might hold curiosities, into rubble.

Fellows load kilns with lime and clay to be fired,

ground, and mixed with water to make cement

for new walls and roads.

Some people want to travel faster.

Mary heads toward the shore.

Joseph turns the other way,

his back straight as the knives

he uses to cut cloth. He's proud

to be an apprentice to an upholsterer,

says, *Chairs are more use than stones*.

Pa taught him to use a hammer and saw.

He used to make fine chairs, too,

though these days wood isn't enough.

Rich folks want soft seats.

Mary passes the brick bathhouses. Children

stack rocks into a tower, dig a small moat.

A brown dog romps past mounds of fishing nets.
Mary has always wanted a dog, though
she knows they don't have food to spare for one.
While villagers hunt for clams and crabs
to make chowder, she checks for cracks
in the cliffs that could warn
of splitting, revelations, or danger.

Much is hidden, like the barrels smugglers stash
behind gorse thickets, or small chunks of coral
that sailors tuck under decks to keep ships steady.
Mary doesn't put faith in such charms,
but if she could make Pa's eyebrows rise
in the old gladly perplexed way, would he get well?
He loves questions as much as answers.
Mary means to find those
he can no longer seek.

Hands

Pa sells his rasps, augers, saws, and even nails
and animal-hide glue. He hoped to fetch enough
for the cost of the church school, but there's just enough
to pay the grocer. Mary doesn't miss school much,
though she wishes she could write more quickly,
even if not as fast as she can think. She'd like to know
more about numbers and the man who found a few fishes
that were enough to feed a crowd. But she can't, and so be it.

She's glad when Pa is well enough to sit up in the bed
in the parlor, which now smells just faintly of sawdust
from the workbench on the other side. Pa gives Mary
and the little boys, who surround him like pillows,
lessons starting with Bible stories. Then Pa turns
an apple like the earth and speaks of a world
round with surprises inside, like an egg or cocoon.

He says their village is special, built on black marl
and mud that once easily took impressions
and held them in limestone and shale.
He spins the bruised apple again and says,

There's more in the earth than anyone knows.
We'll find wonders. Pa twines his fingers
through Mary's, as if she were small again
and needed help on slippery rocks.

Joseph gets up from his perch on a log
sliced flat at the top, showing rings.
Pa says that these stand for the years of a tree's life:
starting from the center, with dark gnarls where the tree
briefly stopped growing or changed direction.

The baby squirms and reaches
for the apple, then grabs Mary's hair.
She pulls down his hand and slaps hers on top.
He laughs, remembering the game.
He slides out his small hand and plunks it on hers.
Mary puts another palm on his.
Pa piles his hand on hers.

Then the whole family plays,
stacking and slipping out hands.

Pa's are nicked from hammers,
Mum's rough from hard soap and water,
and Mary's sun-browned.
All try to keep one on top.

The Empty Basket

Mary shoves open a shutter, sees smoke
rise straight up from chimneys. She says,
It looks to be fair. A good day for collecting.

I don't like you to hunt alone so much,
Pa says. *Go with her, Joseph.*

I must be at the furniture shop, he replies.

Our Joe is better off learning his good trade,
Mum tells Pa. *You might not be in bed
if you'd stuck with cabinets and chairs.*
Her voice scatters like sharp pieces of broken crockery
that can't be repaired, and will be hard to forget.
The baby wails. Mary's little brother sits up, twisting
out of the circle where he slept like a cat on a chair.

Mary says, *I can look by myself.*

*Two is safer. And two pairs of eyes can see
what one cannot. We need the money from the finds.*

Pa needn't add that an apprentice waits for wages.

Mary's little brother loops his thin arms
around his knees and says, *I'm hungry.*

Joseph glances at the basket
people from the church sometimes fill
with stale bread, cheese slivered with mold,
bruised potatoes, or turnip pies. It's empty now.
He winds his woolen scarf around his neck
and opens the door.

Mary struggles into her old coat, now tight at the collar.
She walks behind Joseph as she used to with Pa,
though their silence on the shore isn't the same.
His pace is too quick to see much. His shoulders slump.
She spots a curiosity that's snug between layers of shale,
like a plant pressed within the pages of a book.
She slants her chisel sideways
and taps her hammer to pry it out.

They pass cliffs with varied bands of blue and gray,
shale and limestone layered like the curls in a cabbage

or the fish Mum cuts, on good days, for chowder.
Mary shades her eyes, then scoops her hand
into a circle around them, which changes shadows
or slants of light, and sometimes shows what was hidden.

She feels watched by an enormous eye.
Is that a face in a cliff? Impossible.
No creature has such a long snout full of sharp teeth.
It must be a trick of the light.
Belief is stronger than what's in front of her eyes.

The River

The cottage smells of laundry soap and herbal tonics.
Coughs scrape the air, as if Pa breathes through a grater.
Though Mum swaddles the baby, his whole body trembles
as if he might break. Mary bends over a borrowed
prayer book. Reading isn't just following a sentence
straight forward, but can be a stutter, stopping to muse,
then starting again, following stories past the pages.

At last she puts down the book and pushes past the ropes
strung with damp dresses without patches or frayed cuffs.
She needs to get away from her little brother's clamor,
the baby's tears, the sound of Pa's ragged breathing.

The seaside is where she works. But on Sunday,
she often meets Sarah Jane at the river, where moths
circle yellow gorse blossoms. The girls crush elder leaves
to rub on their hands and necks, leaving a stinky smell
that keeps away flies. To be useful, Mary picks
elder flowers, which Mum will dry and mix
with honey to soothe Pa's throat.

Then the girls play as if they weren't both eleven and should
be practicing being young ladies. For part of an afternoon
they're pirates, members of Robin Hood's gang,
and grown-ups, each with several dogs and no children.

As if Sarah Jane knows Mary doesn't want to go home,
she invites her to her house at the top of the hill.
Her father owns a desk with dozens of compartments
in a room just for writing and thinking about the quarry
where Sarah Jane says he works, though Mary has never seen
rock dust in his hair or the folds of his clothes.
Sarah Jane has her own room for sleeping, as do her brothers
and parents. They have a cook, maids, a gardener, and a parlor
just for needlework, reading, glancing into framed mirrors,
or sipping tea from a silver pot. Sarah Jane has shown Mary
their very own Bible with family names filling a whole page,
all in a row like a spell that keeps them safe.

Mary sinks into a velvet-cushioned chair. Through an open
window, she hears Lord Henley's hounds bay. He owns
the cliffs, the quarries, and the land around them.

Sarah Jane talks about going to his Christmas ball,
where she saw footmen, fruitcakes, custards, and chandeliers.

Mary listens, then decides Pa wouldn't like these stories.
Nothing she does here will make him proud.
She stands up and says, *I have to go now.*

Wishes and Truth

Bees flew inside this morning,
which means fair days ahead, Mum says.
Your pa will get better.

Pa likes sky more than roofs.
But all summer he hardly left the house.
Now he doesn't leave the bed.
The baby coughs and cries at once. Pa coughs, too.

Mary thinks truth is different from wishes.
She won't stop claiming the truth of what she sees
even when what she fears most happens.

After the Last Day

Her baby brother's sock is missing,
but Mary won't bother Mum. She scouts
under beds and in corners, but fails to find it.

The comb is lost too. But they mustn't be late
for church, where all eyes will be upon
the widow and her too-thin children.

After long spells of stillness, there's hurry
in the house, which, like the world,
can change as quickly as lightning
splits the sky, or a last breath is taken.

Back Home

Her little brother asks,
What happened? Is Pa happy?

Mum doesn't look up from washing
the spoon she used to measure medicine,
the cup for tea that smelled like grass.

Mary also chooses silence,
setting soup, when they have it, on the table.

Lost

Friends disappear, too. Why wasn't Sarah Jane at the church
or the graveyard, where Mum left elder branches?
Mary supposes Sarah Jane thinks she's better than her
because she has two names and a house with lots of rooms
and a shiny teapot. But can't moths
in Sarah Jane's perfect house nibble woolen clothes?
Mice might tunnel through any walls.

Even cliffs can crumble. Only rich folks can afford
to pretend much stays the same. They hire maids
to mend shawls and scour stained linen,
gardeners to smash nests and rake gutters.

Mary doesn't need her own Bible to remember
the names of those born and buried. She won't forget.

A Face in the Cliffs

After the rain, Mary walks by the sea,
which seems wide and empty. Pebbles clatter.
A gull drags its broken wing,
its round eyes keeping a calm watch for food.

She joins Joseph, who's walking
below the cliff with the church on top.
Beyond its wide steps, a stone
marks where Pa was buried, then the baby.

Mary bows her head and bends her neck
to break the wind as she walks by Joseph's side.
His gaze stays downward, too, though neither is looking
for anything on the ground. His hands rattle brass
chair nails in his pockets. He says, *I do more
than thread needles for flounces and fringe.
I stitch and stuff mattresses and haul them,
so heavy no one would guess they're full of feathers.*

I know.

Pa didn't know. He never cared about cloth.

*He knew you worked hard. You're famous for matching
not only stripes on the seams of chairs, but checks.*

He shouldn't have died!

Mary doesn't want to cry. She picks up
a stone, flings it into the water.
She throws another
against a blue-gray cliff.
The crash can't be loud enough.

She hears waves spread like claws,
snatching pebbles. Her eyes ache. She reaches
for another stone, aims at a spot
where shale loosens and falls,
then holds back her hand, wondering:
Is that an eye the size and shape of a tea saucer,
faint lines left by a long face? Yes.

The rain must have left a dark shine
framing what couldn't be seen

in strong sunlight or shadows.
A head with a pointed snout or beak is as long as her arm.
Scrambled, shuffled teeth make a jagged line.
Above the mouth is an eye, sun-shaped,
like those of fish or birds, with a patterned rim around.

Mary sets down her basket,
runs her hand along the broken
edge of the thick neck. *Where is the body?*

Joseph says, *It's gone.*

It might be nearby. Or at least part of it, she says.
What breaks can be washed away,
but something so big couldn't have gone far.
She squeezes her hand, tastes salt on her tongue.
She'll scrape away stone.
Wonder doesn't have walls.

The Sea Dragon

About twelve steps away from the head,
but half-hidden under rocks, an animal's skeleton
is imprinted in stone the varied grays of storm clouds.
The body is as long as a barn door or the stone steps
into church. Fins or paddles, patterned
like a turtle's back, jut from its sides.
The end of its tail splits into the shape of a crescent moon.

Mary and Joseph chip away the crumbling stone
around the animal. She leans close to the mouth-filled face
as if trying to understand a difficult voice.
She trails her fingers over the backbone.
It's made of rounded pieces like those that folks
call verteberries, then a shudder of spaces
between ridges shaped by bones. Some spaces
are as wide as those between the tines of a rake.
Other ridges are low, with gaps
as narrow as the teeth of a comb.

At noon, Mary's shadow slides under her feet.
She wonders if this creature raised its head over water

to bellow, silently swaggered, or glided straight ahead.

She looks toward the sea's horizon,

which reminds her of the limits of sight.

Another country lies beyond, or so she's been told.

Some things must be believed without seeing.

And other truths, barely imagined, found.

First

The stone animal is too enormous and strange to keep secret
for long. Neighbors come to gawk, mock, or marvel
at a beast whose length is three times Mary's height.
While she and Joseph chip away the rough rock
holding down their find, the shoemaker asks,
Is that the backbone of a huge crocodile?

Crocodiles don't swim near England,
the schoolmaster's wife replies.
Could it be a thin whale or a monstrous fish?

Or a snake with flippers or wings? Who cares?
the baker's boy asks. *Why are you digging*
it up? You're barmy as the goose girl.

Mary's mother also questions why they waste time
trying to dig out what nobody wants. She says,
We need bread, not stones. Though some folks
crush dragon bones for healing ointments.

Mary brushes aside talk and laughter like dust
as she cuts stone around what most call a sea dragon.

Some claim there's no such thing, or that nothing
that isn't on Earth could have lived here before.
Is it a hoax or sorcery, or do such creatures still swim
under the sea, perhaps near warmer lands?

A well-dressed man from the city asks, *Who found it?*

That would be me, sir. Joseph Anning.

I saw it, too! Mary's heart thuds like hail on stone.

Good work, son. The gentleman doesn't hear Mary,
doesn't see her. He tells Joseph, *I'll give you*
ten pounds for the whole thing once you dig it out.

As they shake hands, Mary slams down her chisel.
No one can measure seeing, name the moment
when lines that plenty of people passed by formed into a face.
If this man is honest and they get paid for their work,
all will go to their family. Mary doesn't work so she can hear
her name on a stranger's tongue, but fair is fair.
Fury is a microscope. She sees more.

Like a Needle

Mum looks at the cliffs with her mouth puckered
as if she ate something sour, though now
that she's heard there could be good money in the find,
she no longer complains about Mary digging each day.

But the gentleman who offered to buy the creature
doesn't come back. Joseph says his words
were a trick. Joseph is tired of rocks and rain.
Most mornings, he cuts cloth at the upholstery shop.
Mary won't stop working through the weeks,
though her hands burn, her scraped knees sting,
and sometimes she, too, gets bored. She keeps on
like a musician who must practice the same notes
over and over, occasionally falling into wonder,
which is like a needle:
small, sharp, ordinary.

Presents

Pence jingle in the pockets of lads running along the shore
to lead gentlemen who rode stage coaches from London
to see Mary and the sea dragon. The gentlemen study
the traces of bones, which are like the lines of a book
with unwritten *whys* springing between the rows of words.

A professor on holiday says, *Animals like these*
may have lived before fire or ice shifted earth and water.
He says that the fossils called thunderbolts
aren't made by lightning strikes. *Other stone seashells*
are found far from the ocean, even on mountaintops.
It seems sea could have turned into earth and flatlands to hills.

Impossible! another man argues,
while Mary considers. Certainty is like a pillow
she learned to live without.
Doubt is crucial. Discoveries are made
by those willing to say, *Once we were wrong,*
and ask question after question. Every one is a gift.

Worth

Joseph spends most of his day stuffing and stitching chairs,
but late one afternoon, he works beside Mary.
Rocks rumble and fall from the cliffs.
They race out of the way.
Her skirt, though she lifts it, gets as soaked as her shoes.

When the cliffs are still again,
they tilt chisels, swing hammers.
She says, *I thought you weren't coming back.*

*I hate it here, but if one fellow thought the sea dragon
was worth something, another may be willing to pay
us still more,* Joseph replies. *I asked your friend
if her father would ask Lord Henley if he would buy it.
He's the richest man around.*

Sarah Jane isn't my friend anymore. Mary stops swinging
her hammer. *And Lord Henley doesn't care about curiosities.*

*He cares about making a profit. He might buy then sell
it to one of those high and mighty London gents.*

She thinks of the stories about Lord Henley's tables
laden with fruitcakes, lemon tarts, and silver pitchers
of cream. She just wants Mum to ladle soup
without counting spoonfuls.

The girl who carries questions as often as a hammer
says, *I want to make money, too.*

Black Shoes with Bows

Mary uncurls her shoulders. Joseph stills his hammer
as Sarah Jane and Lord Henley walk toward them.
Two rows of silver buttons shine on his coat.
He smells faintly of horses, cigars, and dogs.
He studies the sea dragon. Mary looks, too,
then at Sarah Jane's new shoes, which point at the toes.
Bows are on top, though there's nothing to tie together.

I'll pay three pounds for the head, Lord Henley says.
And another twenty for the beast's body, if you can dig it out.

Thank you, sir. Mary's chest swells with the thought
of enough money for food all through next winter,
and perhaps spring. Maybe even enough to buy a dog,
though she believes they'll save instead. No one knows
when or if anything so spectacular will ever again be found.

After Lord Henley leaves, Mary hugs Joseph,
forgetting for now his claim to have found the sea dragon first.
He says, *Thank you, Sarah Jane*.
Mary stays silent. One thank-you seems enough.

Sarah Jane looks down at her pointy-toed shoes.
Mary, it was different back when you collected
sea lilies, even snakestones. My mother says
I shouldn't be around dead things.

They're more than that, Mary says. She doesn't know
how to explain that what's old can start
a new way to see.
She says, *Those shoes are silly.*

Signs

Sweeping the steps, Mary notices the spiderwebs are thick.
Ants scurry. Bees bustle. So she isn't surprised later that day
when leaves turn their pale undersides
toward a cloud-crowded sky.
Birds seek hiding places. Branches snap off trees.
Mary keeps swinging
her hammer as rain pounds on rocks.

Her soaked hair and cloak grow heavier.
Her socks thicken like sponges. She smells like a sheep.
Darkness spreads from air to earth and sea.
Lightning stabs through sky. Rocks tumble, hurtle,
careen and crash from cliffs.
The bells from the tower of the church on the cliff
toll in one long rattling drone,
rather than stick to the usual order of the hours.
At last she braces against the wind and heads home.

After the Storm

The next morning, birds slice a way through blue sky.
Mary and Joseph find broken ledges
covering the spot where the sea dragon used to be.
Joseph spits and walks away.

Tears fill Mary's eyes. But she knows
where to dig. She has time.
She pries away fallen stone,
smashes what can't be lifted,
sweeps off dirt and rubble,
hoping the sea dragon is underneath
and uncrushed.

For weeks she works alone, heading out
straight after breakfast, stopping only
to pet friendly dogs along the way.
She misses her brother, even the arguments
about who first saw a face in the cliff.
Seeing isn't a race,
but is as layered as the rocks.

It's gone, Joseph says, when stopping by
late one afternoon. *It's no use*.

I'll find it, she says, though she's uncertain
as she pries and shovels. Her shadow blends
with Joseph's and lengthens into the cliffs.
Dragonflies dart, as they do before darkness.
She sweeps away dust with a light hand.
Rocks aren't as permanent as they look.

At Last

Mary uncovers the sea dragon. She chisels away
soft stone to bring out the markings of a backbone,
ribs, and what might be flippers or long feet.
She becomes as familiar with the creature as her own body.
No, more. Her tenderness toward the stone is long,
while at home she spends just seconds pulling a comb
through her hair, scrubbing grime from her fingernails,
or tucking her feet into stockings.

She pries out a past that presses up like a wave
that must rise as well as fall. The forces
that left the impressions still seem present.
But will the stone ever budge? Is she wasting her time?
Rock dust fills the small lines on her fingertips.
She misses her father's ponderings, Sarah Jane's stories,
and Joseph. She hears the chime of the bell
by the bathing machine down the shore,
rung when ladies step in the sea, warning
men to keep a distance for modesty's sake.

She's tired. She lies down on the sea dragon,
feeling the bones-turned-to-stone press into her back.

The Tree

While Mary kneels to work, more gentlemen come to look
and discuss whether animals like this might have been
covered with scales. What colors were they?
How big were their brains?
Were they fierce or friendly, nurturing
or freedom-loving, bright or dim-witted?
A visiting doctor who also calls himself a geologist,
someone who studies the earth, says,
This could be millions of years old.

Certainly not millions, another man replies.
The world is only about six thousand years old,
so it says in the Bible, where nothing like this is named.
How dare you question the good book!

Mary keeps aiming her chisel, lifting and lowering
her mallet. She remembers church school and the book
that began with praise of darkness, light, ocean,
birds, and a world made in six astonishing days.
She didn't get far past the second story,
about a woman who didn't mean to start trouble.

Eve loved that tree. How could a hungry person
told that knowledge was close enough to touch
not pick an apple there for the eating?

Mary believes the Lord loves questions as well as answers.
People were given scripture, but also the earth.
She means to read both.

Away

Some of Joseph's friends from the quarry haul
heavy hammers, picks, and crowbars to the site
where Mary finished uncovering the sea dragon.
They smash the stone around it, leaving a margin
about the length of their hands, and dig below it.
The stone sea dragon is finally set free, but it's too long
and heavy for a few strong lads to haul. They decide
to cut it into slabs that can be pieced together again,
like the sheets of rock they slice to build sidewalks.

Mary holds her breath as a chap raises sharp
tools over what she spent most of a year working on.
He slams down a mallet, neatly splitting the stone.
They cut three pieces they lift into wheelbarrows.
They push these to the village and load them
into a wagon, nestling them in straw.

People gather at the town square to bid farewell
as the wagon leaves for London.
Joseph chats with fellows from the upholstery shop.
He stands in back of a crowd including Mum, Sarah Jane,

the shoemaker, the schoolmaster, rogues, the blacksmith,
and cooks from the Three Cups Inn.
While the driver harnesses the horses,
Mary checks the wagon, wonders who left branches
of elderflowers and golden gorse on the sea dragon.

Lord Henley, dapper in his coat with silver buttons,
waves her over. He introduces her to a newspaperman,
who asks, *How did you find this strange marvel?*

Mary looks at Joseph, standing at the back of the crowd.
Is he sorry now that he didn't stick with this work?
No one gathers like this to cheer for a chair.
She says, *My brother saw it first.*

The newspaperman dashes over to Joseph.
The horses shift their hooves, then start to pull
the wagon up the hill. Little boys whoop.
Mum laughs as a little girl calls good-bye and
does a cartwheel. Sarah Jane hands Mary a sprig
of gorse. She smells faintly of elder leaves.

Thank you, and for telling Lord Henley
about what we found. Mary looks down.
Your shoes aren't really silly.

I'm afraid they are, Sarah Jane replies.

Mum looks at the cliffs with an unpuckered mouth,
as if she finally knows that like cures hidden
in plants, stone holds treasure, too.
She tucks a loose strand of hair behind
Mary's ear and says, *Your father would be proud.*

New Words

Waves flatten back to water.
As seasons and years pass, Mary imagines
the world's past and her future. She comes to call
ancient stones *fossils*, as scientists do,
scraped clean of old superstitions.
She learns that snakestones are called *ammonites*,
thunderbolts are *belemnites*, lampshells are *brachiopods*.
Brittle stars are *echinoderms* and devil's toenails are *gryphaea*.
What Mary thought of as a sea dragon is proclaimed
the first *ichthyosaur* ever discovered.

Names and knowledge change, the way the turning
world brings color or deep shadows, without a sound
even as soft as the twist of a key in a lock.

The Fossil Finder
1840

Mary and her mother move to a cottage away from the bustle
of the boot-maker's and butcher's shops, the jail,
and the house where Joseph and his wife now raise a family,
closer to the meadows where Mum likes to walk.

Mary seeks bigger and more peculiar stones than those
that fit on the old round table she still keeps by the door.
The longer she looks, the more the earth speaks,
though the language is inexact. She adopts
a black-and-white dog who follows her everywhere.
She knows the tides like the pulse of her own blood,
but it's good to hear Tray whimper warnings
before waves come too close.

Mary finds fossils of great swimming creatures,
including the first plesiosaur ever seen,
with a long, sinuous neck and tail.

She digs out a wide-winged pterosaur
that astonishes members of the Geological Society.
Such a strange flying creature has never been found in England.

Gentlemen pay handsomely for these.
Some resell the fossils for more
in London, where they're displayed in cases
or mounted on museum walls. These days,
Mary trades more in pounds than pence,
but still some winters she fears the poorhouse.
Unlike the upholstery shop,
where Joseph's chairs are regularly wanted,
finding and cutting stone
is an unpredictable trade.
She depends on weather and chance.

As she looks for stones, scholars seek help from her,
though she left school when she was ten, about thirty years ago.
She hunts and chisels, but also reads complicated reports.
She makes intricate drawings,
dissects squid and cuttlefish,
comparing their insides with feathery lines fanning
from what seem like spines on fossils of similar forms.
She weighs old theories, draws new conclusions.
Claiming this world, Mary claims herself.

Waves curl back to their beginnings,
shaped like the spirals of snakestones,
or the faint whorls marking finger pads,
or the centers of eyes.

Many Hands

Shrieking gulls soar over stone and sea.
They cast shadows over two people whose silhouettes
show top hats, like the one Mary now wears. It's sturdier
than a straw sunbonnet, keeping her safer from tumbling rocks.
She greets the men who came from the city to talk with her,
walking past cliffs where storms have uncovered
gray stone streaked with blue bands, layered
like the pages of a book, twined fingers,
or the stack of hands over hands
in the game her family played long ago.
Do these strata of earth, like the rings
in a tree trunk, mark history? Could the earth
be not just thousands of years old, but millions?

Mary blinks. She brushes rock dust from her eyes
with hands hardened from swinging a hammer.
Her left shoulder slants down from all the years
of lugging a satchel filled with a hammer, chisels,
and stone. She imagines the sea dragon,
the ichthyosaur, lunging through waves. She looks
up as if startled by the shriek of a pterosaur,

spreading batlike wings over the sea where,

perhaps, plesiosaurs once swam swiftly,

lifting their heads over seaweed,

before disappearing from the earth, leaving

only impressions of their bones.

Even marks of waves on wet sand

can turn to stone.

What's lost is found again.

Many Stars, One Comet

Maria Mitchell

(1818–1889)

The Mapmaker's Daughter
✣ NANTUCKET, MASSACHUSETTS, 1831 ✣

Maria Mitchell (pronounced ma-RYE-ah) often worked with her father to make star charts that helped sailors travel more safely on the sea. Maria's favorite work took place on a flat part of the roof, where she looked through a telescope at the moon, planets, and stars. She observed patiently and taught herself mathematics to further an understanding of the night sky.

Three on the Roof

The sky dims, its blue thickens.
The pale moon grows bold.
Maria and her father stand on a flat, fenced platform
on the roof. Living near the edge of an island,
Maria is as familiar with sky and sea as land.
Her eyes slowly adjust to the dark.
Night vision is dulled by looking
from the sky to paper, so as Father peers
through the telescope and names what's half hidden,
she checks charts and records numbers.

The click of her counting tongue is broken
by footsteps on the ladder in the attic.
She steps back to make room for her older brother.
Father asks him, *Did you come to help?*

Starlight reflecting on the ocean makes it bright enough
to see Andrew frown and Father's smile fall.
Then Andrew grins at Maria. Maybe he understands
she goes to the roof for what it brings to her
as well as Father, both caught by the same questions.
Andrew says, *I found work.*

Congratulations, son. What is it? Father looks down
as if the line of jobs he's suggested form a rope between them.
His oldest child could be a teacher, farmer, or cooper,
make soap and candles, repair watches, or keep bank accounts.

It's honest work. Andrew shoves his hands
in his pockets, jangling two knives, like those sailors carry.

We'll talk tomorrow, Father says. *I need to finish
some calculations for a ship that will sail early tomorrow.*

Maria usually prefers two people on the roof.
One to watch the black sky. One to write on white paper.
But as Andrew backs down the ladder, it seems too quiet
under stars whose light no one can touch.

Morning

As her sisters set fried codfish, toast, crab apple jelly,
and plenty of plates on the table, Maria asks,
Is Father already out making maps?

*Yes, at the end of the island. He hardly slept after staying up
to correct a chronometer,* Mother says.

What's that? Phebe asks.

You've seen them, Maria tells her little sister.
Captains bring them to Father to fix.

Oh. The boxes I'm not supposed to touch.

They're fragile. They show ships where they sail.
Maria notes another empty chair. She picks up a kettle
as it shrieks. *Did Andrew go with Father?*

Both were gone when I got up at dawn. Mother reaches
over the twin babies on her lap to wipe the little boys' faces.
Maria, please fetch some thread and pins at the general store.

Maybe you'll see some sign of Andrew in town.

Maria nods. Phebe says, *I want to go, too.*

Maria thinks Phebe will walk too slowly, but doesn't argue.
Mother looks worried. Maria wonders what was hidden
behind Andrew's short sentence about finding work.
Should she have spoken? It's not the place
of a twelve-year-old girl to tell father and son,
who've been at loggerheads for months, to talk.

Maria tries to hurry Phebe past the silk mill,
the candle factory, and the shipyard, where men
sing or swear as they saw and stain pine logs
shipped from Maine for masts. The girls join
a cluster of cousins on a wharf crowded
with folks watching men shinny up masts,
getting a ship set to leave. They unfurl sails
and shout with Irish brogues and Southern accents,
or in languages Maria doesn't understand.
One man has a gold hoop in his ear and an eagle
tattooed on his neck. Sailors from India sport turbans.
Several boys about Andrew's age, sixteen,

wear blue checkered shirts
that are loose at the shoulders,
sewn to still fit when the growing boys return.

They scramble up rigging, sling their bodies over spars.
Maria spots a boy in a plain Quaker-gray shirt that fits
precisely over his narrow shoulders. He's Andrew's height.
His hair, dark as hers, sweeps his shoulders as he ducks
behind a sail. Is it her brother? Did he mean to hide?
She raises her arm to wave, smiling
as if sighting a star just where she expected it to be.

Sails snap. From the deck, the captain calls,
Haul up the windlass! Heave ahead!
The ship plunges forward. With bow piercing blue water,
it's easy to forget that the ship could be gone
for a year or three, depending on weather and whales.

Phebe adds her small, high voice to those on the wharf,
shouting, *Godspeed! Fair winds!*

Maria's belly hurts. Should she have shouted?
Would the boy have looked or kept pulling lines

strung to spars and sails, with the joy
she feels when turning the lens of a telescope
so the night sky, more brightness than black, comes close?

The ship skims through the sea, churning ripples
of foam. Soon she can't tell the sails from the sailors,
who must be shouting, singing, climbing, and watching
clouds for signs of how the wind will change.

Gingerbread

A string of small bells above the door chime.
Maria and Phebe enter the store stocked
with rolls of calico, penny dolls, rakes, and
barrels of fragrant pickles, chestnuts, and apples.
There are buckets of tar and boxes of tea and nails.
One glass jar holds raisins, another
colored beads, a penny for a thimbleful.

Phebe pauses before a case filled with red-and-white
peppermints lined up on paper, a glittering mound
of rock sugar candy, and rows of gingerbread.
She lifts her chin to see the squares on the top shelf
with star-shiny glaze, which cost half a cent more.
Then her eyes catch on something silver. She asks, *What's that?*

A harmonica. It makes music, Maria says.

That's wrong. Only three years old, Phebe already knows
good Quakers don't play pianos or fiddles.
Her gaze returns to the gingerbread.

'Tis a waste to wish for what we can't have.

Maria asks the clerk for pins and brown thread.

Her belly feels heavy as she looks away from the mail sacks

hanging from rafters marked with destinations:

North Atlantic, Cape of Good Hope, Pacific Ocean, Anywhere.

Phebe wanders to a case of silk ribbons,

which, like fancy buttons or bows, are forbidden.

She says, *I wish my hair were curly.*

That's foolish, Maria says, as a twelve-year-old must

to a sister nine years younger. She doesn't say,

You're already pretty, or, *Sometimes I wish that, too.*

Supper

Inside the house with its clapboards split and peppered gray
by salt air, the Mitchells hold hands around the table.
Maria's mother and older sister wedge babies under their arms.
The little boys, Frank and Forster, stretch their arms
to span the gap over an empty chair.
At the end of the silent prayer,
Mother gives one of the warm, wiggling twins to Maria,
then spoons out clam chowder, slices rye bread.

Where's Andrew? Frank asks.

Facing the crisscrossing straw on the empty chair,
Maria says, *I think I saw him on a ship leaving the harbor.*

He wouldn't do what I forbid. Father's face reddens.
Maria, are you certain of what you saw?

No. Maria knows it's important to be precise.
But last night he said he had work.

He said he was leaving? And no one told me?

Mother blinks, as if remembering
the way Andrew practiced tying knots
and memorized which lines to coil,
which sails to furl in a storm.

Far Away

Maria hears the night watchman pace past their house,
ringing his bell, while keeping an eye out for anyone
breaking curfew. No one wants to stumble into gates
on moonless nights or trip in holes dug by dogs,
but Maria finds more beauty than danger in night.
Nantucket warehouses are stocked with barrels of whale oil,
but most will be sold off-island, where less-thrifty people
put up streetlamps. Maria is glad her neighbors are frugal.
Even lanterns in windows can wash out darkness
and dim the lights in the sky.

While Mother settles the twins,
Maria tucks Phebe into the bed across the room.
Failing to be a good sister to Andrew,
not calling for him to come back, she vows
to be good to Phebe. They both bow their heads
for silent prayers, the kind taught by Quakers,
who encourage questions but set many rules.
They may skate on the frozen bay and attend
cornhusking and sheepshearing festivals,
but they don't dance, play cards, or hang frilly curtains

or pictures on plain walls. Quaker women
don't stitch lace on collars or cuffs, or curl their hair.
They wear linen clothes instead of cotton, and sweeten
food with honey, never sugar, to protest
slave labor on Southern plantations.

Phebe says, *If I'm good, God will bring Andrew home*.

Maria knows she should say, *The Lord works
in mysterious ways*, a pretty way to say that people can't always
have what they choose. But she stays silent.

Playing Planets

Schoolmasters don't make much money, so Father earns more
by walking around the island to take measurements for maps
that mark shorelines and shoals. Maria suspects he also asks
relatives for news of Andrew, who disappeared last week.

While Father is gone from his schoolroom, Maria arranges
primers, chalk, and slates. Taking out the wooden spheres
to give an astronomy lesson, she remembers Father holding
the largest ball, bringing the sun to their parlor.
The children ran around him like orbiting planets, taking turns
as Saturn, Mars, Mercury, Venus, Jupiter, and Uranus.
Holding a baby, Mother was Earth.

Maria loves how planets take measured places in the sky,
but also hold mysteries. Once, she wished she could be a comet,
soaring close to the sun to be seen,
appearing as if from nowhere
among the whirls of sisters and brothers,
her father steady in the center.

Number One Vestal Street

The little boys chase the cat across the parlor floor.
Frank waves a fireplace poker, calls, *There she blows!*
Ho! Look yonder, men!

Aye, aye, timberhead! Forster jumps on a chair.

Put that down and sit still, Father says.

Put that down, Phebe repeats, shaking a small stick
with a charcoal tip she used to draw on the hearthstone.
You're not Andrew on a whale ship.

Silence follows the name that hasn't been spoken
since their brother left last month.
Maria asks, *Father, may we go to the roof?*

I want to come, too, Phebe says.

The little boys also tag along, through the attic
and up the ladder. Everyone finds places, elbow to elbow,
on the platform surrounded by a fence,

what some people, though no one on this island,
call a widow's walk, as a nod to women who watch
for ships and men that don't always come back.

Father snuffs out the lantern.
A pale moth flutters away.
I'm going to wish on a star, Phebe says.
I can't tell you what I wish. It's secret.

Maria looks up at fixed stars, which keep spaces
between one another, orderly as a set table
before plates are filled, spoons picked up.
Frank and Forster beg to use the telescope, but
Father won't let anyone look beyond a few peeks
until they learn enough mathematics to understand
depth and distance. He points at stars and says,
They're fiery and huge, casting their own light,
like the sun, which is bigger than all the planets put together.
But stars are small within the galaxies,
which are billions of stars that are small
within the universe.

Maria likes trying to fathom such numbers, but Phebe fidgets.
Maria crouches, points to a constellation, and whispers,
Doesn't it look like the dipper we use at the well?

Phebe doesn't speak, but squirms.
Maria wraps an arm around her.
She wonders about the sides of the moon and planets
no one can see.
She says softly, *You're kind to make a wish for Andrew.*

You're not supposed to say his name. Phebe stands more stiffly.

Maria whispers, *It's all right if we say it to each other.*

Sisters

The full moon's bright light fades the view of stars.
Maria goes to the roof anyway. Father uses the moonlight
to split wood. She hears his ax strike frozen logs.
Dogs bark. Owls hoot. The longer she looks, the more
she sees in the blue-black sky brimming with history,
calendars, and maps for sailors and other wayfarers.

She goes down to the room she shares with two sisters.
Sally is two years older, and Anne two years younger.
Their heads tilt toward each other's.
Maria lifts the quilt at the bottom of the bed.
She squirms into her place, nudging her sisters
slightly to the side, slipping her still-stockinged
feet toward their shoulders. The space between them
is already warm. Pairs of feet frame her cold ears.

She hears soft steps coming from the chamber
where the twins cry. She shifts to make room for Phebe,
who snuggles close and whispers, *I miss Andrew.*

I know. Now that the harbor is iced over,
there's no chance of news until spring.

Waiting is worsened with tales of pirates
and lanterns that tipped and set fire to decks.
She's heard about whales gone mad,
sailors washed overboard by enormous waves
and others who lost their balance on spars or masts.
Ships could crash into icebergs, flood, and sink.
It's not uncommon for a ship to get lost
in a storm, or wash up on sandbanks or shoals.

He should have said good-bye, Phebe says.

He didn't want Father to tell him to stay.

Father told him to stay.

Sometimes people must do what no one else understands.

Will he come back? He gave me rides on his shoulders.

I can do that, Maria says, though she knows
it's not the answer Phebe wants. She stretches
her still-chilly hands toward warm ones,
a constellation of sisters in one bed.

Kinds of Silence

No one speaks as the family enters the meetinghouse,
but Maria sees worshippers glance past Father's shoulders,
as if they can't help noting the space
beside him where his oldest son used to stand.
Here there is no stained glass, statuary, organ,
minister, priest, or even a pulpit.
The Mitchells sit on wooden benches on a morning
most call Sunday, but these Quakers call First Day.
Disapproving of the days and months
being named after pagan gods,
they call January First Month rather than invoke
the two-faced Janus. Maria wonders if they forgot
to rename the planets. She's glad they let them be.

Here in a narrow room, perched on narrow benches,
they wait to hear small, holy voices speaking from within them.
They're patient as those hoping to spot a rare comet
among the predictable planets and stars.
On one side sit boys and men in black hats.
On the other, girls and women wear gray bonnets.
Maria prefers the undivided sky.

Saved

Waves pound louder than the rain that splashes
against the wharves, where men tie up fishing boats
brought in early. The wind flings a rake.
Flowerpots tumble across yards.
Maria hopes the storm will stop tonight,
as rain blocks a view of stars.

After supper, she sets the ladder-back chairs in a row
and sweeps the floor. As the curfew bells ring from a steeple,
Maria sits by Mother, who darns stockings.
Her older sister knits and talks
about dances Quakers can't attend.
They only skim or sashay. Pointing one's toes isn't wicked.
Sally's hands twist yarn and the memory of patterns.
Maria knits, too, for everyone needs socks,
and at least the work exercises minor mathematics:
counting and making geometric adjustments to toes and heels.
But she hates embroidery, its worth measured
by the smallness of stitches. A needlewoman trains
her eyes to stay cast down while hiding knots and boredom,
committing herself to the circumference of a lap.

Later, Maria helps Father clear a space on his desk covered
with scavenged bird nests, seashells, a few garnets,
and fossilized shark teeth. He opens a chronometer
to tinker and tighten. No one on Nantucket is more trusted
to set each small part in place. Father teaches Maria the uses
of spiral springs and the winding pin, which powers the clock,
and how the balance wheel stores and releases power.
A chronometer must stay steady no matter the weather.
Spindled gears push a small lever that measures seconds.
A longer lever moves more slowly, marking minutes.

When the rain stops battering the windows,
she and Father carry quicksilver and a sextant
to the roof. They measure the height of stars,
used to tell the longitude, or how far
a ship is between continents,
so sailors can know where they are. That can save them
from shipwreck, particularly if night or fog hides land
no one thought was near. Precise calculations could save
a boy like Andrew, whose name they still don't say.

At the Breakfast Table

Mother reaches for apples where they're tucked
to keep cool in the space between the wall and ceiling.
She pares them for pie. Father opens a newspaper,
turns past the page with the black-lined box titled *Disasters*.
He reads from an article about how the king of Denmark
offers money and a gold medal to anyone
using a telescope to spot a comet not yet seen.

You will! No one knows the sky better, Maria says.
She imagines a comet's clouds of ice, rocks, and dust
hurtling closer to the sun, where some ice melts,
making mist and a long sash of light.

Aren't comets unlucky? Frank asks. *I heard
they foretell earthquakes, explosions, or plagues.*

Those are foolish old tales, Maria says. *Comets soar
and circle back, though we can't always see them.*

I want to see an earthquake. Or an explosion, Forster says.

The prize could make our fortune,
Anne says. *Father could be famous.*

We don't seek glory, Father says. *Besides, it's not likely*
anyone in America would see a comet before astronomers
in Europe. They've built better telescopes.
And night falls there first.

But if a cloud covered a comet over Europe,
here along the coast we might see it blaze first.
Maria is glad stars follow certain courses. Still, she wishes
a comet never before seen would startle through sky.

The Letter

Mother pins clothes on the line strung between trees.
Sally's dress is tied loosely above her ankles
to keep it from billowing as she wrings shirts over a washtub.
Maria and Anne make sure the small, curious twins
keep away from the flames warming the water.
Maria shows them that if they lie
on their backs, they'll get the best view of sky.

The twins play near the garden, which Father used to cherish
but this spring left to the girls
to plant beans, cabbages, and carrots.
Past the plot's borders, clover and wild roses lure bees.
After one twin is stung and the other won't stop toddling
toward the steamy water, Sally takes them inside the house.
Mother asks Maria to go to the windmill to buy cornmeal
and to the general store to mail a letter.
She hands her an envelope addressed:
Andrew Mitchell, South Pacific.
She says, *I'm told that's where that ship was headed.*

Maria knows that this letter will be put in a canvas sack
and carried to the next ship heading south and around

Cape Horn. But it still might not reach Andrew.
Sometimes a ship will steer toward another
and exchange mail sacks to be passed along.
Yet ships may sail out of each other's sight
more often than they stop.
And even when letters reach shore, their readers only know
the sender was alive when the words were written.

I should have tried to stop Andrew, Maria says.

No one can stop a ship meant to sail. Mother's hands
smell like good soup. She must have been weeding
the sage and thyme. *If it's anyone's fault that Andrew left,
it's your father's and mine. We named him after your grandfather.*

Maria has heard how Mother met Father
when he came to her house looking
for pumpkin seeds that her father had brought
on a ship returning from South America. The grandfather
Maria never met didn't come back from his next voyage.
Mother fell in love with the young man who wanted
to plant seeds instead of sail. Even now, she won't bake

pumpkin pie or pudding, as if such seeds weren't worth
the risk of a ship gliding into the harbor with sails at half-mast.

Mother squeezes Maria's hand. *It's not surprising*
that someone growing up on an island
would want to know the sea all around us.
I just wish we'd had a chance to say farewell.

The Harbor

Hearing the town crier call that a blue flag has been raised
over South Church, Maria and Phebe hasten
past narrow streets, lanes, and alleys. They reach the wharves
and warehouses, which smell of cinnamon sticks,
sandalwood, gingerroot, and molasses.

Beyond the brickyard, barrel-making shop, sail loft,
and bakery, a ship is newly anchored in the harbor.
Sailors with skin the color of pinewood, teak, or mahogany
unload casks of whale oil. The deck is piled with blubber,
bundles of whale bones, and baleen that might be carved
into walking sticks, fans, shoehorns, corset stays, umbrella ribs,
buggy whips, fishing rods, and butter knife handles.

No boy wears a plain Quaker-gray shirt.
No face brightens into familiarity.
Maria hears small boats rock and knock against the wharves,
tugging on ropes that hold them.
She says, *Andrew could be on the next ship*.

Phebe has heard this before. She asks,
Will Father cheer when he comes back?

Of course. Maria shifts from one foot to the other.

Truly, she doesn't know if Father will forgive

him, offer that fresh chance. She folds her hand

around a coin he gave her for teaching. *Let's go to the store.*

I have a cent. You can get gingerbread with glaze.

She's sick of scrimping and rules that keep no one safe.

If only she had enough to buy Phebe a ribbon.

Truly, wishes are never wasted.

Telling Time

The next morning, Maria lets the blankets stay rumpled.
She won't smooth them over sheets tucked in crisp corners.
After breakfast, she pushes the chairs back to the wall
but leaves the line crooked. Her father is away again.
Maria is not sure she likes how the world
both insists on order and isn't always reliable.

When she hears a tap on the door,
she expects someone has work:
Most neighbors, aunts, and cousins don't bother to knock.
She lifts the latch and greets Captain Chadwick.
His wide arms are wrapped around something the size
of a loaf of bread, swaddled the way men carry
chronometers to protect the delicate gears.

Mother, whose belly is now moon-shaped, bustles in.
She says, *I'm sorry, Mr. Mitchell isn't here. He's taking
measurements of shorelines on the other side of the island.*

Criminy, Captain Chadwick says, then more softly,
I beg your pardon, ma'am. When will he be back?

Tomorrow or the next day.
He stays with relatives when his work lasts long.

I don't have a day to tarry. The tides and weather
look fair to sail soon. No one else
in Nantucket is as trusted to rate a chronometer.

Maria *can do it, Mother says.*
She's just thirteen, but her father has taught her well.

The captain peers at Maria. 'Tis true I've heard
that Mr. Mitchell's daughter has a head for calculations.
Can you promise every number will be right?

Aye, sir, I won't miss my reckoning. Maria knows
split seconds, which add up over many miles, matter.

When the captain leaves, she says, *I've never fixed*
one without Father watching.

And now you will, Mother says. He would not have told me
you've become as capable as he is if it weren't true.

That night on the roof, Maria opens a sextant.
It's silver and about the size and shape of a hand
with fingers pressed together toward the earth,
and a thumb pointing to the sky.
This holds a small telescope, which she aims at a star.
She sets a metronome, its beat soft as prayer, to count
the seconds the star takes to move across a bounded field of sky.

She brings her notes downstairs to Father's desk,
where she twists tiny wheels, adjusts bearings, tightens springs.
The clock in the case keeps Nantucket time,
which sailors can compare with the time on deck
to learn their location, factoring in how the earth
rotates fifteen degrees every hour. Maria concentrates
to keep out the sounds of Phebe and the boys convincing
the cat to explore mouseholes. Sally complains
it isn't fair that she can't dance with young men who wear
medals won for harpooning their first whales.
Mother frets over the crying twins.
Henry and Eliza are so sick that she, usually frugal,
says that she'll light the fireplace in one upstairs room.
She hums lullabies. *I know 'tis wrong to sing,*
but if I can bring them small comfort, I shall.

Maria braces herself against the noisy parlor, leans on numbers

that must be exact, in rows strict and straight as brooms.

At last she tucks the timepiece among wheels

that will keep it steady while a ship rolls on waves.

After everyone goes to bed, she dozes in a chair,

then climbs back through the scuttle to check the sky again.

She hears birds, frogs, and wind rustling through

the bayberry shrubs, the racket of crickets,

while measuring angles between stars,

the horizon, and where she stands, on a roof she loves.

All Hers

Boasting is wrong, but when Father returns home,
Mother sounds proud as she tells him
about Maria's excellent calibrations. Father's smile
is never large, but Maria sees its slim crescent
as he finds a saw, hammer, and nails
and gets to work to build a small room under the stairway.

This room fits just a chair between one wall and a desk,
where Maria puts her treasury of mathematics.
This is happiness. She closes the door
and tends to calculations, trying to shut out
the sounds of the boys pretending the stairs are a ship.
Ho, gluepots! Look aloft! Make sail!
The terribly ill twins often cry, a ragged wail,
though Mother's footsteps as she paces sound even.
Phebe comes in to ask Maria to stitch a doll dress.

Later, the good sister paints a sign for her door:
Maria Mitchell is busy. Do not knock.

Winter Sky

Because numbers calm her, Maria counts
seventy-six ships anchored in the harbor,
with no more likely to come until spring.
She runs home past turned-over rowboats and
the graveyard. Ice coats the ropy vines left behind
by grapes and leaves, the prickery brown brambles of roses.

Inside the house, Frank and Forster don't play
that they slaughter whales. No one takes out the checkerboard
or suggests they tell riddles or play charades. Only Henry,
who's well now, asks for stories. He's too little
to understand he won't see his twin sister again.

The fire in the hearth burns quickly as wind whooshes
down the chimney. Everyone but Maria goes to bed early.
She puts on three pairs of woolen stockings
and four flannel petticoats, claps on earmuffs,
winds a scarf in orbits around her neck,
and drapes a shawl over her shoulders. She carries
the telescope, a broom, paper, a pencil—since ink
would freeze in its bottle—and a lantern up through the scuttle,

which smells of dust, spiderwebs, some sort of eggs
and cocoons. The cat skulks behind.
Her green eyes dazzle like jewels.

The moon is bright, having been struck
by winter's strong sunlight.
Maria sweeps snow from the roof.
She hears a gate, wind-whisked off its hinges, clatter.
Bricks topple from chimneys and thud on the ground.
She braces for cold as she peels off her thin mittens
to turn the telescope so a star
is in the center of the crosshairs marking the lens.

When gusts from the sea turn particularly strong,
she plunks a rock on the frost-covered paper
and flings herself flat on the roof
so she's not blown over, then observes again.
She often hears her mother walking below
as she tends to unsettled sleepers, but now
footsteps tap on the ladder. Phebe clambers to the roof.
She says, *I didn't want you to be lonesome.*

I'm not. Maria looks up to the stars
crowding the sky. *Go back to bed.*

The sky is bigger at night, Phebe says. *It's scary.*

It's beautiful. Maria loves how the darkness
goes on and on, like wonder,
in a sky thick with secrets and stars.

The Universe

Inside her small room, Maria pores over her notes
on magnitude, distance, and angles between stars.
She checks charts of stars and nebulae:
clouds of dust and starlight.
She calculates orbits, ellipses, and gravitational forces.
The numbers and formulas are as necessary
as a telescope for understanding the sky,
though not everything can be answered
by drawing lines as straight as those made when sweeping
an iron, slicing a beach plum pie, cutting patches for a quilt.

She loves the elegance and economy of mathematics,
which can pry open the view of the heavens,
splinter ideas that have been held for thousands of years.
She's fond of formulas that mirror
nature's love of curving lines,
seen in seashells, plants that rise and bend back,
birds building nests, orbits of planets,
even truth, which spirals in and out of sight.

Trespasses

Maria opens the door to her room under the stairs,
knocking the chair. Mother stands up.
Startled, Maria steps back.
It's strange to see her mother here and without a child
in her arms or beside her. Her eyes are red-rimmed.

Mother says, *I'm sorry. I shouldn't weep when I've been given*
so much. A house full of children.
The Lord works in mysterious ways,
but I wish I knew why He took our little girl.

Maria wants answers for everything, but supposes
she'd sound like a heathen to say so. She knows
that in a sky full of stars, each one, singly, matters.
She opens her arms, which don't reach all the way
around Mother's hard, round belly.

Mother runs her sleeve across her face,
eyes the stack of library books. Maria remembers
Mother telling her that she worked in a library
before marrying Father, and read every volume.

Now she scarcely finds time
for a poem or two.

Mother's eyes land on the ink bottle, knocked over
by the chair or the hug. She blots up the stain
as best she can. She says, *This is a good room,*
but it's yours and I'm glad. I shan't come in again.

Maria watches the back of her mother,
who surely has never broken a commandment,
though one seems small: *Thou shalt not covet.*
Maria is certain that some wanting can't be wrong.

The Harmonica

A new, healthy baby wails from the second floor.
In the yard, Maria rescues half-drowned beetles floating
in horseshoe crab shells that her brothers brought home.
She empties Henry's pockets of pebbles, dried milkweed pods,
and blueberries. Henry is still so little that he spreads his arms
when he runs. He hasn't learned to clutch a pen, but asks,
Where does the sun go? Why does the moon change shape?

Phebe draws in the dirt, stopping when bells clang.
The town crier shouts news of a blue flag on the church.
So often they've heard this and gone looking for Andrew.
Maria is tired of disappointment. Still, she calls to Sally
to watch Henry, who was just a baby when Andrew left.
Has anyone told Henry about the brother he can't remember?

Maria, Frank, Forster, Anne, and Phebe rush
down Main Street. Rows of elms cast
short summer shadows by the newspaper office,
the courthouse, a tavern, and the big bank with its flat roof.
They reach the wharves, which smell of salt water, tar, and fish.
Smoke rises from the shop where blacksmiths forge
fishing hooks and harpoons.

Gulls drop and drag shadows over sailors
scrambling down ropes or planks.

Maria rises on her toes as if spotting a red bird,
the first yellow flowers after a long winter, or a comet.
There's a boy wearing a plain Quaker-gray shirt.
It's tight at the shoulders. This boy
is taller and tanner than when he left.
Maria's brothers and sisters shout Andrew's name
like a long-practiced song they can finally sing.

After untangling arms, Frank asks, *Did you kill a whale?*

No, but I was first to spot one. Here's my prize.
Andrew reaches in his pocket, takes out two knives
and a harmonica. It seems a small silver silent thing
to bring back from such a long voyage.

That makes music, Phebe says. *God doesn't like that.*

*Sailors need songs to keep in step while we haul lines
or scrub decks.* Andrew crouches to talk to her.

Father says, No music in our house, Phebe says.

Andrew unbends his knees. His hands stiffen,
his wrists bare beneath sleeves that are now too short.

Let's go home, Maria says. As they walk,
she tells Andrew about the small girl who died.
And Mother had another baby girl.

Maria fixed a chronometer for Captain Chadwick,
Phebe says. *Father gave Maria her own room.*
She has a sign that says to keep out.

The room is little and under the stairs. Maria laughs.
Skipping isn't against Quaker rules,
but she knows she's too old for such.
Still, she must keep pace with children
romping to the far end of Main Street.

At One Vestal Street, she sees Father chopping wood.
Mother and Sally drop the wash they're hanging
and rush to hug Andrew. Father puts down his ax.
His mouth makes a line as taut as rope in wind.

Andrew turns the way he did on the roof the last time
he was here, and walks into the house.
Maria, Mother, Sally, who's holding the baby, Anne, Phebe,
Frank, Forster, and little Henry follow him into the kitchen.
After Mother cuts corn bread and pours cool sassafras tea,
Father enters. He stoops in the doorway.

Andrew saw a whale, Phebe says.
He won a harmonica. God doesn't like it.

I don't suppose we can always know what the Lord likes.
Father looks at Andrew. *Would you play it, please?*

Andrew lifts the small instrument to his lips.
The sweet notes of a sea song rise. For the first time,
music is no longer secret between the unadorned walls.

Maria touches the top of Phebe's head, imagining
ribbons on her braids. Maybe one day
they'll even twist their hair into ringlets or curls.

New Desks

Will there ever again be such amazement as that music
in their house? Maria wonders. She won't go whaling,
but listening to Andrew's stories, she wishes for other ways
to see what's beyond this island, though she find marvels here.
After tending to chores such as cooking, cleaning,
and keeping her little brothers and sisters out of scrapes,
Maria climbs to the roof. Perhaps one day she'll see
an uncharted comet curve past constellations.

She teaches more of her father's classes, then at seventeen
starts her own school. She teaches reading and arithmetic,
then takes her students to bogs, cliffs, or tide pools
to study starfish, sea moss, butterflies,
and fossils of teeth or small bones.

Soon Sally marries. Andrew finds work fixing watches.
Father takes a job as head cashier at the bank, and the family
moves to its second floor, under a flat roof
with plenty of room for the telescope
that Maria turns each night,
alert to all that's familiar and any slight change.

She closes her classroom when she's offered a job
at the new library, called the Atheneum.
In the morning, Maria studies.
She means to master intricate mathematics
in between helping neighbors choose books.
She keeps records of which titles come and go,
as well as the day's weather: the temperature inside
and outside the library, cloud formations, and wind directions.
She tucks her ledgers in the northeast drawer of the desk.
She arranges talks, and sorts and shelves books, taking volumes
with outdated science to the dim attic. There she finds cocoons
she brings home for Phebe to draw, along with wildflowers,
fossils, and seashells. Her life is good.
She tries not to want more.

Night Watches

After dark, Maria focuses on the particular colors and pulses
of stars. She keeps an eye out for comets, watching as patiently
as a sailor who might win a pig, a jug of cider, or a harmonica
for being the first to spot a whale.
Comets could carry clues if not answers to questions
such as *Where do they come from? Where will they go?*
Will they orbit back? and *Is there life beyond this planet?*
Maria knows the sky so intimately now that she'd recognize
the slightest change. She must look at the right moment,
though the more time spent on the roof,
the more luck is possible.

Her father's telescope is the best on the island,
necessary for the maps he still makes of land and sky.
But Maria sighs when one crosshair on the lens splits,
then another, which makes it hard to measure.
Father offers to bring the lens to Boston or Cambridge,
but she hates to miss a few nights of looking
while he rides a ferry, then waits for the repair on the mainland.
Could she make a new grid herself, using one of her own hairs?
She plucks one but finds it's too coarse. She experiments

with the fine hair of Sally's baby, but it curls in the cold.
Magnified by the lens, such a crook could cover
her view of a star.

Striding past the mulberry trees by the silkworm factory,
Maria remembers spotting a cocoon under the library roof.
She plucks it from a rafter and unwinds the silk. Working
with the delicate strands, sealing wax, miniature screws,
and brass plates, she constructs a new grid on glass.

Once again, she takes her time sweeping her telescope,
slowly as a painter shifting the tip of her brush,
or a girl scanning stones. Beauty rambles more than it rushes.
There's always more than what's first seen.

Chance

Fog. Clouds.
Maria recognizes the two nebulae in Ursa Major
but not what seems to be a third
—or a ghost, sheen, or smoke—between them.
Could it be, behind clouds, the tail of a comet?

The next night she measures angles
between the known nebulae, near the Dolphin.
The telescope pulls stars closer, smudging the invented lines
of constellations, revealing patterns visible to practiced eyes.
But more clouds make precise calculations impossible.

The next evening, whatever she saw is gone.

Discovery

Slipping a book onto the wrong shelf, Maria scolds herself.
She pushes her thoughts back to the alphabet
but can't help being eager for darkness.
Could a blur she saw yesterday, five degrees north of Polaris,
be there again? Comets move fast but are so far away
that she might bend by a telescope for hours
to see traces of motion.
Will the day's clouds vanish? Will the night be clear
enough to see what's not in the star atlas?

At last she shuts the library door. The coming evening
stretches shadows, brings out the scents of wild asters
and goldenrod she picks for the table,
fragrances that day's warmer air kept close to Earth.

She returns to the second floor of the bank building.
She's lived here about ten years with the family,
which is smaller since Andrew stopped repairing watches
and left to sail around Cape Horn, this time to California
to look for gold. Maria dusts the piano she and her sisters
bought with savings and smuggled into the house.

Their parents agreed that once the piano was up the stairs,
it seemed too large to bring back. Not much later,
Maria gave up the old Quaker rules. She wants to curl her hair
and sew curtains with frills, but she still believes
what her father carved on a plank kept in the attic:
An undevout astronomer is mad. Her brothers and sisters
used to balance on that plank, pretending it was a ship
or undiscovered island on the sea of the dusty floor.

In the kitchen, Maria fries bluefish, mixes corn pudding,
sets the table with plates and dishes of wild cherry jelly.
She greets guests and makes conversation, telling no one
what she might have seen the night before.

Shortly before eight o'clock, she slices blueberry pie,
pours tea, and excuses herself from the table.

On the roof, her pupils slowly widen to let in more light,
revealing the pale green, orange, yellow,
purple, sapphire, and red hues of stars.
The church bells chime nine times, then ten.
She knows the sky as well as her own self,
yet feels uncertain as a new light sails in a curve

like the back of a whale, a bending blade of grass.
Through the lens, the crescent-shaped haze
is shorter than the edge of her smallest fingernail.

She may be mistaken,
or she may have found what's uncharted.
She backs down the ladder and walks slowly
to the dining room, holding hope
carefully as a china cup that could spill.
She smiles at guests slicing second or third slivers of pie,
smells the gold and purple flowers she put in vases,
the bayberry candles, as she bends to whisper to Father.

He stands, excuses himself, and joins her on the roof.
She says, *Maybe someone else has already seen
it in Europe. It will be weeks before word can cross the sea.*

At the telescope, Father lets his eyes adjust to darkness,
then says, *You found a new comet. We must send out notice.*

Names

After Maria receives the gold prize from the king of Denmark,
first offered seventeen years ago, Father boasts
of her as if she were still a girl, not turning thirty.
He enjoys introducing himself as Miss Mitchell's father.
The medal is engraved with her name on one side and the muse
of astronomy on the other. Maria tucks it in a drawer.
Gold won't help her to see anything new, and it seems strange
to be honored for one instance of seeing, rather than thousands
of nights on the roof, memorizing what's constant in the sky
so she could recognize change when it came: Comet 1847 VI.

Maria is reminded that it's a tradition for comets
to be named both with letters and dates
and after those who discovered them.
She sought knowledge, not glory. She was raised to be humble.
But it's one thing to ask modesty of men with a history
of honors and trophies, and another for women to step
to the back row. Miss Mitchell's Comet belongs to all seekers
who want to know the names of women who persevered.

The Wider World

Maria adds her prize money to what she's saved
to travel around the country, give talks, and see night
from new longitudes. Then she sails
across the Atlantic to meet astronomers and visit
observatories and museums in London and Paris.
She takes the train to Florence and admires statues of Galileo.
In Rome, she looks at ancient shrines and art during weeks
of waiting for permission to become the first woman to enter
the Vatican Observatory, where she's told to leave before dusk.

Some call Maria a phenomenon. Others find her odd.
She returns to the island, where wives, sisters, and daughters
chop logs, saw planks, hoe fields, or keep shops
while men are away on whalers.
There, a daughter who helped her father
at a telescope seemed ordinary enough.

She earns honors and is the first woman elected
to join the American Academy of Arts and Sciences.
The women of America collect money to buy her
a better telescope. She gets a chance to use one even finer

when she accepts a position as the first female professor
of astronomy at one of the first colleges open to women.

She says good-bye to her brothers and sisters, all married now.
Phebe gives art lessons. Frank is a tinsmith.
Forster teaches former slaves. Henry surveys land.
Maria packs her books, her curling iron,
her china teacups painted with pictures of astronomers,
jars of beach plum preserves, and bayberry candles,
which smell sweeter than lamps, though the light isn't as steady.

Maria's mother has died, but her father comes with her
to Vassar College, where he's been given a room.
Maria sleeps on a cot under the observatory's sky dome.
She likes using the tall telescope and teaching
young women, but she's bothered by parents
who fret that advanced mathematics might strain
their daughters' delicate constitutions.
She says, *My mother had ten children
and did more night work than most astronomers. We'll be fine.*

The deans are determined to show that educated young ladies
are still ladies above all. They set rules such as *No sewing
on the Sabbath.* Students are warned not to cross their ankles

and risk showing their shape, or to sit sideways on their chairs.
For dinner, they must change from gingham dresses to silk,
and when biting into bread, be vigilant not to leave a vulgar
horseshoe shape. All letters must be approved by authorities.
When a dean asks Maria if she might use the telescope to see
if a student left the grounds, Maria refuses its use as a spyglass.
She won't take attendance or give grades.
She's an astronomer, not a warden or judge.
She tells her students to be curious, to do their best,
and to ignore small rules, such as those about lights-out.
They must break curfew and join her for work
that begins after dark.

Under the dome, where Maria teaches for twenty years,
she looks up and wonders: Why do stars flicker,
brighten and dim? How old are stars? How far away?
She lifts her long dress to climb the ladder
to the telescope that's often cold,
for it must be kept the same temperature as the outside air.
She shows her students how to recognize the motion of meteors,
signs of the sun's rotation, and the phases of Venus.
She teaches them how to use meridian instruments
and locate the positions of planets at any time of day.
They study sunspots, solar eclipses, and the surfaces

of Jupiter and Saturn. They measure the angles of shadows,
drawing lines that meet at the top, like the shapes of sails.
They marvel at how light takes a long time to reach the earth,
revealing that the universe is older and, like truth,
more immense than first thought.
Standing straight as a telescope,
Maria says, *Trust your own eyes*.

Stars flash and fade from sight.
A woman's name once widely known may vanish,
but never entirely or forever disappear.

A Note from the Author

S ome girls have always cared about half-hidden lives in woods or meadows, and the ways stones and stars reveal the past or open views of the future. Maria Sibylla Merian, Mary Anning, and Maria Mitchell explored what's hidden: the origins of caterpillars, the earth's history as written in stone, and what can be seen in the sky only with telescopes. They all knew people who were afraid of insects, or the possibility that gigantic animals lived in the past, or the vast distances of space, but these girls were curious and brave. All three were brought up with a strong religious training and found ways to honor their beliefs while pursuing scientific truths. Most jobs, colleges, and scientific associations were then closed to women, but Maria Merian, Mary Anning, and Maria Mitchell fought or found ways around discrimination. Part of their lasting strength came from their fathers' encouragement to trust their own eyes.

During the times when the people in this book

lived, what we call science was often thought of as an appreciation of the natural world, a suitable subject for anyone. As technology developed, many scientists focused less on observing land, water, and sky and more on what could be recognized only with intricate equipment. As science became more specialized and respected, women became increasingly excluded. Of course some persisted, including the magnificent Marie Curie and the women she taught and inspired at the Radium Institute she founded in Paris. After Marie Curie visited the United States in 1921 at the invitation of women's groups raising money for her experiments, the number of American women earning advanced degrees in chemistry and physics increased dramatically. Sadly, after her death, the number went down again.

Even today, girls who enjoy observing animals, planting beans in broken eggshells, drawing the parts of flowers, or lying on their backs to watch the night sky may come to feel unwelcome in high school and college science classes. The percentage of young women compared with men in higher-education science courses drops, and too few female students land jobs as researchers or professors in technology, invention, or medicine.

This is sad and wrong. As Maria Mitchell pointed out in 1875, "science needs women." I wrote *Finding*

Wonders in the hope that girls, and open-minded boys, would become more familiar with those who devoted their lives to raising questions and seeking answers.

History often focuses on the triumphs of individuals, but most scientists work with others, and different people may discover almost the same thing at around the same time. Maria Merian was among those who were challenging the old idea that butterflies were born spontaneously from mud or rotten vegetables. She painted pictures that became highly valued for the way they illustrated changes from eggs to caterpillars to chrysalises to adult butterflies or moths. She may have been the first person to sail across the sea for purely scientific reasons. In South America, Maria Merian painted an amazing variety of plants and animals. These stunning pictures, now displayed in museums, helped educate naturalists in Europe about life in a different climate and became the basis for more studies.

The hundreds of fossils Mary Anning found helped her and others read the story of the earth in stone. She became the first person known to make a living by selling fossils. Although she wasn't trained in biology or geology, she helped bring about important new ideas, and continues to be an inspiration for those without scholarly training to pursue knowledge.

The gold medal that Maria Mitchell won for spotting a comet brought her fame and many invitations to speak. She accepted a variety of important positions, including becoming the first female professor of astronomy at Vassar College. She was determined to see that more young women had chances to work in science.

Knowing our history can make us stronger. The three women in this book were all famous in their time. Honors included caterpillars named after Maria Merian, extinct species named after Mary Anning, and the comet bearing the name Miss Mitchell. While some facts have been passed along, many memories of these women have turned faint. History tends to capture moments of discovery, so we miss much of what came before and after, including common experiences that may bond us.

I chose to write in verse because of the permission it gives me to fill in what disappeared. I read biographies, letters, science books, social history, and field guides, but when answers couldn't be found, I drew from details to imagine scenes and the girls' inner lives. I learned key events, such as that Maria Merian raised and sketched silkworms at age thirteen, was taught to paint by her stepfather, and would marry and later separate from his apprentice, then I invented between the lines. We know that Mary Anning's father taught her to find fossils and died after a fall, but the circumstances of first seeing an ichthyosaur fossil have been told in varying versions; here I created my own. After learning that

186

Maria Mitchell corrected a chronometer at age thirteen when her father wasn't home, and that her brother ran away to sea, I relied on imagination to depict her family's responses to these events. As if working with raw silk, I tried to honor the character of what I was given, while spinning out facts into verse. I pass it along to readers who I hope will look for other books, as well as wonders of the earth, sea, and sky.

Reading Past These Pages

As you explore the books listed here and do research on the Internet, you might remember that biography may be approached not just with a name, but from a slant. I read all I could find about the scientists in *Finding Wonders*, but also about news from when they lived. I studied pictures of old houses and neighborhoods, what people ate and wore, seventeenth-century silk mills, and nineteenth-century hammers and telescopes. I also looked at present-day video clips of splitting cocoons and photographs of fossils and comets.

I love words, but what we see tells stories, too, which is why I believe that picture books aren't only for those who can't yet read on their own. The best biographical picture books are like poetry in that every word counts. Readers may ask: What do the pictures tell about the person and setting that the words don't? How do these few pages suggest what's most important about a life? What's left out that another writer might want to put in?

Writers of picture book biographies must decide how much to include about the life of a subject as a young person and how much about her as an adult. How many scenes will be included and how much summary? Deciding how much time to cover is like choosing between taking a close-up photograph or one with a long view.

In *Summer Birds*, Margarita Engle focused on thirteen-year-old Maria Merian's understanding of metamorphosis, with a clear sense of how her love of beauty and science merged. *Maria's Comet*, by Deborah Hopkinson, centers on Maria Mitchell's curiosity about the sky, which began as she grew up in a big and close family. All three women in *Finding Wonders* were famous in their day, but reliable records are scarcest for Mary Anning, whose formal education was limited. People she met wrote some impressions of her, but some of what was passed along seems more mythical than true. Those of us who have written about Mary Anning had to sort out what sounded most probable and make decisions about the importance of Mary's memory of her father, how and where the first ichthyosaur fossil was found, and with what balance of persistence and good fortune Mary began her extraordinary career.

While few books for middle-grade readers focus

entirely on these scientists, their stories can be found in collections focused on courageous women. I wrote about Maria Merian in *Girls Who Looked Under Rocks: The Lives of Six Pioneering Naturalists*. Information about Mary Anning is often included in books about fossil discoveries. Maria Mitchell's life story can be found in books celebrating women astronomers, as well as *Maria Mitchell: The Soul of an Astronomer*, by Beatrice Gormley, and *Maria Mitchell: Astronomer*, by Dale Anderson. More information is available about Maria Mitchell than the other women here, perhaps since she lived most recently; or perhaps because as one of the first professional librarians, she understood the importance of saving documents. She gave her papers to her sister, Phebe Mitchell Kendall, who compiled them into *Maria Mitchell: Life, Letters, and Journals*.

Books written for adults that were crucial to my understanding include Kim Todd's compelling and thoroughly researched *Chrysalis: Maria Sibylla Merian and the Secrets of Metamorphosis*; *Maria Sibylla Merian and Daughters: Women of Art and Science*, by Ella Reitsma; and *A Butterfly Journey: Maria Sibylla Merian, Artist and Scientist*, by Boris Friedewald, which is the shortest of these and perhaps the best introduction. Collections with reprints of Maria Merian's paintings are also great to study and enjoy.

A good overview of Mary Anning's life can be

found in Shelley Emling's *The Fossil Hunter: Dinosaurs, Evolution, and the Woman Whose Discoveries Changed the World*. Books about the early years of fossil finding also reference the work of this trailblazer.

Sweeper in the Sky: The Life of Maria Mitchell, by Helen Wright, is filled with lively detail. *Maria Mitchell and the Sexing of Science* puts her life in the context of women's place in the history of science. Renée Bergland shows how scientific fields were more welcoming to women back when much was based on observation of the natural world, before science became more specialized and lucrative. The author follows the progression of Maria Mitchell's college students finding good work to increasing discrimination toward women in science during the twentieth century. In 2005, Lawrence Summers, at that time president of Harvard University, suggested that women were underrepresented in the sciences because they didn't have the natural ability. The outrage that followed this speech helped open new paths for women in science, technology, engineering, and mathematics.

It's time. As young women today make places in the STEM fields, I hope they'll remember the ways that Maria Merian, Mary Anning, and Maria Mitchell kept room in their lives not only for the gifts of science, but also for those of art, stories, poems, families, and all the wonders of nature.

Selected Bibliography

*Books noted with * were written for young readers.*

Maria Sibylla Merian

* Atkins, Jeannine. *Girls Who Looked Under Rocks: The Lives of Six Pioneering Naturalists*. Illustrated by Paula Conner. Nevada City, CA: Dawn Publications, 2000.

* Engle, Margarita. *Summer Birds: The Butterflies of Maria Merian*. Illustrated by Julie Paschkis. New York: Henry Holt, 2010.

Friedewald, Boris. *A Butterfly Journey: Maria Sibylla Merian, Artist and Scientist*. Munich: Prestel Verlag, 2015.

Reitsma, Ella. *Maria Sibylla Merian and Daughters: Women of Art and Science*. Oxford: Oxford University Press, 2008.

Todd, Kim. *Chrysalis: Maria Sibylla Merian and the Secrets of Metamorphosis*. New York: Harcourt, 2007.

Mary Anning

* Anholt, Laurence. *Stone Girl Bone Girl: The Story of Mary Anning*. Illustrated by Sheila Moxley. New York: Scholastic, 1999.

* Atkins, Jeannine. *Mary Anning and the Sea Dragon*. Illustrated by Michael Dooling. New York: Farrar, Straus and Giroux, 1999.

* Brown, Don. *Rare Treasure: Mary Anning and Her Remarkable Discoveries*. New York: Houghton Mifflin, 1999.

Cadbury, Deborah. *Terrible Lizard: The First Dinosaur Hunters and the Birth of a New Science*. New York: Henry Holt, 2000.

Emling, Shelley. *The Fossil Hunter: Dinosaurs, Evolution, and the Woman Whose Discoveries Changed the World*. New York: St. Martin's Press, 2009.

McGowan, Christopher. *The Dragon Seekers*. Cambridge, MA: Perseus Publishing, 2001.

Maria Mitchell

Albers, Henry, ed. *Maria Mitchell: A Life in Journals and Letters*. Clinton Corners, NY: College Avenue Press, 2001.

* Anderson, Dale. *Maria Mitchell: Astronomer*. Philadelphia: Chelsea House, 2003.

Bergland, Renée. *Maria Mitchell and the Sexing of Science*. Boston: Beacon Press, 2008.

* Gormley, Beatrice. *Maria Mitchell: The Soul of an Astronomer*. Grand Rapids, MI: Eerdmans, 1995.

* Hopkinson, Deborah. *Maria's Comet*. Illustrated by Deborah Lanino. New York: Atheneum, 1999.

Kendall, Phebe Mitchell, comp. *Maria Mitchell: Life, Letters, and Journals*. Boston: Lee and Shepard, 1896.

Wright, Helen. *Sweeper in the Sky: The Life of Maria Mitchell*. New York: Macmillan, 1949.